A LEGACY FROM TENERIFE

By Noah Webster

A LEGACY FROM TENERIFE

NOAH WEBSTER

PUBLISHED FOR THE CRIME CLUB BY
DOUBLEDAY & COMPANY, INC.
GARDEN CITY, NEW YORK
1984

Library of Congress Cataloging in Publication Data
Webster, Noah, 1928–
A legacy from Tenerife.
I. Title.
PR6061.N6L4   1984   823'.914
ISBN 0-385-19556-7
Library of Congress Catalog Card Number 84-4117

First Edition in the United States of America

For Winifred and Geoff

"Estates, heritable and moveable, fall as *bona vacantis* to the Crown as *ultimus haeres* from various causes. This can include moveable property in Scotland of foreigners who have died intestate. . . ."

H.M. Exchequer Office

"If it doesn't belong to anyone else, it belongs to us."

A former Queen's and Lord Treasurer's Remembrancer, in conversation

A LEGACY FROM
TENERIFE

CHAPTER ONE

It was the kind of night in February when anyone with even a half-decent excuse stayed indoors and was glad. Edinburgh had spent most of a cold, dull Monday just recovering from the weekend, then snow had begun falling as the early winter dusk arrived.

Two hours later, at 7 P.M., snow was lying several inches deep and the Scottish capital had been brought to an undignified standstill. Trains stopped running from Waverley Station, the airport closed, every suburb had its quota of stranded buses and abandoned cars. A young cop in Corstorphine acted as midwife when a woman gave birth to twins in a snowed-up taxi. Then he fainted. Two girls won a bet by skiing down the Royal Mile dressed as penguins. A fanatical activist on his way to plant a bomb at a political rally in the Usher Hall slipped, fell, blew himself up, and demolished the roof of a public lavatory. The political rally had been cancelled anyway.

Over it all, a stark Gothic silhouette on a fantasy white wedding-cake of rock, Edinburgh Castle scowled down on a Princes Street where only the occasional vehicle still struggled past the steadily blinking traffic lights.

Jonathan Gaunt didn't give a damn.

He was home in his apartment on the west side of the city. He had got there after work at the Exchequer Office while the roads were still brown slush. His only plan for the evening centred round half a dozen scratched but playable old jazz 78's, all recorded long before he'd been born. Gaunt had discovered them in a junk-shop off Leith Walk.

If you respect vintage 78's you play them with a freshly sharpened hardwood needle. Gaunt had a small, cherished stock, teamed with a modern Japanese rack system and an adapted pick-up arm. The result also needed some extra filter channels, but was good. Jack Teagarden pulsed an improvised blues number with a reasonable minimum of hiss and crackle, at sufficient volume to fill the slightly shabby but comfortable little two-room apartment.

The cheese omelette he'd been tending was ready. Gaunt eased it onto a plate, dumped the pan to wash later, and brought the plate through from the kitchen. There was enough left in a bottle of Muscadet to fill a glass and he poured it, sat down, then began eating.

The Teagarden number ended in a monotonous rasping whirr. Gaunt changed it for an even scratchier but rare Earl Hines, lowered the pick-up arm by hand, waiting for the first few notes, then returned to his chair. Lounging back, he sipped some of the wine, listened to the jazz piano washing over the room, and relaxed.

Jonathan Gaunt was a tall man, in his early thirties, with a compact build, a slightly freckled, raw-boned face, and untidy fair hair. He had moody gray-green eyes, the kind which gave a hint of an occasionally stubborn temperament. Because he didn't plan to go anywhere, he was wearing faded denim trousers and an old sweater which had a hole in one elbow.

He felt content, something that didn't happen too often.

First, there had been the weekend—which had meant Janey.

Janey had raven-black hair, was in her late twenties, and was a surgical nurse. She'd been part of the team at the army hospital where he'd arrived as Lieutenant Gaunt, Parachute Regiment, his back broken but still lucky to be alive after a partial chute failure. It had been long months before he mended and even then the long haul wasn't over. There had been things like being told by Patti, his young, blond wife, that she could now tell him she wanted a divorce. Things like the army notifying him he was being invalided out, discharged unfit, the verdict reaching him the day after the dull formality of the divorce hearing.

But Janey had kept in touch. A year to the day later, she had arrived, dumped her overnight bag inside the apartment door, and announced she had come for the weekend. From then on, it happened every now and again.

On the practical side, he even had a little money to spare—and that was rare enough. For once, his small-time stock exchange gambling had paid off, he had recouped most of his losses of the previous six months.

He'd risked half the previous month's pay-cheque on shares in an apparently terminally ill manufacturing company because he had heard that a group of visiting strangers had been given the red carpet treatment. Ten days later, the shares had soared on a take-over bid. He sold out and suddenly, unbelievably, had a bank statement which didn't show an overdraft.

But the practical came second. His thoughts strayed to Janey again. They were two normal people, she was more than a friend, but neither of them wanted beyond that. It might be months before he saw her again; that was Janey's way.

Earl Hines came to a raunchy finish. Gaunt drank the last of the wine then checked the next 78 on the pile. It was an old Bessie Smith classic with a Columbia label, scored and useless on one side but looking surprisingly fresh on the other. It took a moment or two to resharpen the hardwood needle with a slip of emery paper, then Gaunt set the record turning and went to lower the pick-up arm.

The telephone rang. Cursing mildly, he crossed the room, lifted the receiver, and answered.

"Jonathan?"

"Yes." He knew the voice only too well. Henry Falconer was senior administrative assistant to the Queen's and Lord Treasurer's Remembrancer and as an external auditor Gaunt was several rungs lower down the department ladder. He liked Falconer, but when Falconer called him at home it was seldom good news.

"I'm snowed in," said Falconer unhappily. "How are things with you?"

"I don't know," admitted Gaunt. "Probably not so bad." He knew Falconer's home, on the outskirts of the city close to Edinburgh Zoo. He'd also met Falconer's wife, a hard-faced, demanding woman. The unkind said that Falconer lived close to the zoo so that his wife could see her relatives more often. "Anything wrong?"

"Yes. There's a problem." Falconer sighed. "It needs something done, and now. You'll have to turn out."

"Tonight?" Gaunt winced at the thought.

"Tonight," said Falconer. "I can't, you're nearer—"

"And I'm supposed to be fronting for you at a meeting in Amsterdam tomorrow," Gaunt reminded him.

"If the airport is open, yes," said Falconer. "This will only take an hour or so, and it won't interfere with the Dutch thing. Anyway, the department file behind it is coming your way." He broke off, his wife's voice sounding sharply in the background. There was a muffled silence, as if Falconer had put his hand over the mouthpiece, then he came back on the line, his voice lower and slightly strained. "Look, Jonathan, I've also got a certain amount of domestic friction happening at the moment. If you remember what that was like—" He stopped short, embarrassed. "I'm sorry. That wasn't tactful."

"Don't let it worry you," said Gaunt drily. "What's gone wrong?"

"Here?" Falconer was surprised.

"No," said Gaunt patiently. "The other thing."

"I've a meeting scheduled for tomorrow with a Canadian woman who is over here; I haven't met her, but she made contact with us." Falconer paused. "Now I've had a call from the police. She was robbed at her hotel this evening; I don't know the details. But she seems to have some crazy idea we might be involved."

"That's a good start." Gaunt knew the sarcasm was wasted.

"Her name is Mrs. Lorna Anderson, she's a widow, from Vancouver, and she's at the Carcroft Hotel," said Falconer, unamused. "She's bad news. Soothe her down, pat her on the head—whatever is needed."

Falconer's wife interrupted. There was a repeat of the previous silence, but longer.

"Where was I?" Falconer came back on the line. "Yes—get to her, do what you can. She's some kind of genealogy freak, an ancestor hunter, and she came over from Canada about three weeks ago to do some research on her family tree. Her particular branch left Scotland generations back, but she believed she might have one relative still alive over here."

"And?" So far, Gaunt had heard the same kind of story several times over.

"And she found him," said Falconer. "A man named Peter Fraser who died last year—we took his estate for the Crown as *ultimus haeres*."

Gaunt whistled. "And now she wants it back?"

"Yes. She may be genuine; I'm not sure yet." Falconer was impatient to finish. "So show we care, emphasise we're ready to listen— but don't promise anything."

"If I can get to her," warned Gaunt. "I may need a sledge and dog team."

"That makes two of us," said Falconer and hung up.

Bessie Smith was still spinning idly on the turntable. Gaunt switched off the player, then went over to the window and looked out. The snow was falling steadily, nothing moved in the street, the few parked cars had become lumps of white.

A few minutes later he was driving through the blizzard, in towards the city.

Driving. To be handling a car of his own again was sheer poetry.

His last set of wheels had been sold to prevent a long-suffering bank manager going critical. There had been a gap of months before these industrial shares had cleared his overdraft, cleared it and left enough to spare for the down payment on an accident-damaged bargain. Less than a year old, it had been sold when the previous owner lost his licence after failing a blood-alcohol test.

The car was a small black two-door hatchback Ford Escort, the high-performance XR3 version with Bosch fuel ignition. The accident damage had been fixed for him by a disabled army veteran, an ex-sergeant who ran a repair and tuning shop in one of Edinburgh's back streets. They'd worked on it together, shading down the already lowered suspension, breathing an extra edge into the 1600-c.c. engine's four small cylinders.

After that, the XR3 had shown an ability to accelerate from thirty to seventy mph. at a stop-watch time of under eight seconds. Gaunt had found there was road-holding to match. If it was possible to really love a car, he decided, this was it.

But tonight it was enough of a struggle just to keep moving, wipers battling to clear part of the windscreen, wheels scrabbling for grip on the soft, treacherous surface.

Half a mile from the apartment, the main road was blocked by a stranded truck. Gaunt managed a U-turn, made a detour, then swore as two pedestrians appeared out of the white murk, walking blindly towards him.

Braking wouldn't help. Saying a prayer for the Ford's freshened paintwork, he heaved at the wheel, dropped from top to second gear, and gunned the engine. Tyres clawed for grip, the car slewed and swung, then bounced as it met an invisible kerb. Scattering snow, shaving a lamp-post, he caught a final glimpse of the two pedestrians in his rear mirror. They were plodding on as before.

But at least when he got to Princes Street, snow-ploughs and gritting trucks were at work. Crunching in their wheel-ruts, he managed to make a turn and reach Rose Street. Then, after another turn, he partly tobogganed down an incline to stop outside the Carcroft Hotel. Leaving the car, he hurried across into the shelter of its lobby.

The Carcroft wasn't imposing. It was one of several Edinburgh hotels which existed on the middle-income bed-and-breakfast tourist trade. The lobby carpet was threadbare, the decor was a mixture of excursion posters and souvenir showcases, and the reception desk was positioned under a moth-eaten stag's head which had only one glass eye.

Gaunt caught a glimpse of himself in a mirror. He was wearing a black leather jacket over a brown tweed suit and an open-necked white shirt. There was snow on his hair and on his shoulders. Maybe he should have worn a tie. But at least he'd made it.

"I'm here to see Mrs. Anderson," he told the red-haired girl behind the reception desk. "She's expecting me."

"Well—" The girl hesitated and looked past him, giving a quick, beckoning gesture. A tall, middle-aged man with a horse-like face stopped considering one of the showcase displays and ambled over.

"You want to see Mrs. Anderson?" he asked in a bored voice.

Gaunt nodded.

"Any identification?"

"Yes," said Gaunt. "Have you?"

"Police." The long face flushed and a warrant card appeared briefly. "Detective Sergeant Angus."

"Remembrancer's Office," said Gaunt and showed his own plastic-sealed identification. "Thank you, Sergeant."

"Just routine," said the policeman defensively. "Your boss doesn't want any kind of publicity, Mr. Gaunt—and the hotel feels the same way." He indicated the elevator. "I'll take you up."

Gaunt followed him into the old-fashioned iron basketwork cage. The door clashed shut and they creaked two floors up. Then they stopped, Sergeant Angus heaved the door open, and led the way down a badly lit bedroom corridor. He stopped at one of the doors and tapped with his knuckles and it opened. A younger man looked out, nodded a greeting, and stood back as they went in.

"Detective Constable Dunn," said Angus. "We're all that's here."

The hotel room was small. It was also a chaos of emptied drawers and scattered clothing, the sheets dragged from the bed and the mattress overturned.

Gaunt turned as he heard the door close behind him.

"Where's Mrs. Anderson?"

The two policemen exchanged an awkward glance.

"She collapsed on us," Angus said uncomfortably. "We were half-way through getting a statement from her and she just keeled over."

"Like that," said the younger policeman and snapped his fingers. "Like she blew a fuse."

"I see," Gaunt chewed his lip. "Where is she now?"

"In hospital," said Angus. "There's an Australian doctor staying in the hotel. He took a look at her, said it was some kind of heart attack, and we called an ambulance."

"An aunt of mine died that way," murmured Dunn. "It was at a wedding—too much excitement."

"Dangerous things, weddings," said Angus caustically. He turned back to Gaunt. "Mrs. Anderson is in the intensive care unit at the Royal Infirmary. I called them a few minutes ago; she's still unconscious, but they think she might make it."

"When did it happen?" asked Gaunt.

"About half an hour ago," Angus said. "I phoned your boss again and told him."

"I'd have been on my way here by then." Hands in the pockets of his leather jacket, Gaunt stood silent for a moment, looking around the ransacked room. "What about this lot?"

"Well, I wouldn't blame room service." Angus gave a mirthless grin. He had large, yellowed teeth which made him look more horse-like than ever. "A plain, ordinary piece of sneak-in hotel thieving. As a crime, it's on the increase—and this place is made to measure for it."

"Why?"

"Most of the guests are tourists, they leave after a few days and another lot arrive. Tourists go out and about, so the rooms are deserted in daytime. There's such a turnover of faces that anyone could walk in and out without being noticed."

Gaunt nodded. It sounded reasonable enough.

"Who discovered this had happened?"

"She did—Mrs. Anderson." On surer ground, Angus leaned back against a wall and relaxed. "She told us she'd been out most of the afternoon. Then the snow delayed her, and she didn't get back until well after six. She'd left the room locked, and it was that way when she got back." He paused and gestured at the door. "Locked? Breathe on a lock like that and it would open. Chummy would only need five minutes then he'd be on his way out again."

"He was thorough enough." Gaunt walked around the hotel room, feeling a strangely detached anger at the way it had been left. Underwear dumped from a drawer had been scattered over the carpet. A padlocked case had been slashed open across the lid and more clothing thrown about. Even the contents of a make-up bag hadn't escaped, and a bottle of nail varnish had been smashed. The contents had hardened as a blood-red pool on a white silk blouse. "How much did he get?"

"He—or they," said Angus. "They sometimes work in pairs." He scratched his chin. "Just some junk jewellery and her camera; that's all, she reckoned. Have you met her?"

Gaunt shook his head.

"She's in her sixties—"

"Sixty-three," said Dunn.

"Sixty-three," agreed Angus wearily. "A bright little terrier of a woman, maybe a bit odd, but nobody's fool. Uh—you know about the long lost relative?"

"Who happens to be dead?" Gaunt nodded.

"Yes, she told us." Angus eyed Gaunt slyly. "She also reckoned your Remembrancer's Department were an illegitimate gang of thieving vultures; that's toning it down a little." He produced cigarettes, put one between his lips, but left it unlit. "Anyway she was smart, or lucky, or both. She has a damned great haversack of a shoulder bag, with anything that matters to her stuffed into it. She had it with her."

Gaunt was at the window. He looked out, but all he could see was the hotel backyard, the dark outlines of other buildings, and snow. He thought how it must be to be elderly, to be a long way from home, and to come back to the kind of chaos around him. He felt the anger come again.

"Where's her bag now?" he asked, turning.

"It's here." Angus ambled over to his companion. "Dunn, how about doing something useful? I could use a cup of coffee; they'll have some somewhere."

Dunn nodded and left them. As the door closed behind the detective constable, Angus made a slow business of producing matches and lighting his cigarette.

"Any time I feel like a private talk, I want it really private," he said ponderously. "Like—well, right now, Mr. Gaunt. Here we've got a pretty ordinary little hotel theft. But Mrs. Anderson made some wild-as-hell suggestions about documents and your department—"

"Never on Mondays," said Gaunt. "Wednesday is our breaking-and-entering day. Or did you believe her?"

"I believe trouble when I hear it," sighed Angus. "That's why I contacted my divisional boss. He felt the same. That's why he gave me your boss's home number and told me to let him know."

"Then it was my turn." Gaunt looked around again. "Were any other rooms touched?"

"No." Angus couldn't find an ashtray and used a flower vase as a substitute. "The hospital desk asked me about next of kin. Do you—?"

"Sorry." Gaunt shook his head. "Maybe you should try the shoulder-bag."

"I was thinking about that." Angus seemed pleased at the suggestion. "The Aussie doctor rummaged it anyway, to see if she was on any kind of medication." He went over to the wardrobe, reached up to the space above, and brought down a large, old-fashioned bag made of well-worn cowhide. "But she'd create hell if she knew about this."

The bag had a simple brass latch. Angus opened it then raised startled eyebrows at the crammed interior.

"Women!" he said feelingly.

They cleared a space on top of the dressing-table, Angus upended the bag, and its contents came spilling out in an untidy heap. Sighing, he handed the bag to Gaunt and began sorting through the collection. Gaunt checked the bag again. It had two zip pockets inside. He found a purse and lipstick in one; the other yielded a thin fold of travellers' cheques, an airline ticket, and a Canadian passport.

Muttering to himself, Angus was still busy. Gaunt opened the passport at Lorna Anderson's photograph and looked at it for a moment. It showed a woman with neatly styled grey hair, a thin, lined, but potentially cheerful face, and intelligent eyes. She looked the way Angus had said: nobody's fool.

He closed the passport. Angus was still sorting through the handbag's contents and pushed two spectacle cases and a small first-aid kit over to join a suede jewellery case, a set of keys and three different colours of headscarf.

"Look at this." Angus picked up a small, tartan-clad souvenir doll. He shook his head. "Thank God men only have pockets."

"Usually with holes in them," said Gaunt absently.

He turned to another collection Angus had set to one side. A notebook, two large, bulky envelopes, and some old, faded photographs in a plastic folder were held together by a thick elastic band. Another envelope, smaller and separate, was sealed. He picked it up. Across the front, in small, precise handwriting, was the instruction "Only to be opened in the event of my death. Last Will and Testament of Lorna Anderson."

"Better keep that safely." He pushed the sealed will across to Angus, then picked up the bundle and removed the elastic band. "I'll try these."

The two large envelopes were unsealed. Both seemed to contain collections of yellowed documents and other papers. He decided not to disturb their contents, took a quick glance at the photographs in the folder, mostly faded family snapshots, then tried the notebook. It was the spiral-backed type and pages appeared to have been torn from it as they were used. Any that remained were blank.

But there was something on the inside cover. He took it over to where there was more light. A heavy inked circle had an exclamation mark added above it.

"Found something?" Angus joined him.

"Maybe." Gaunt growned at the words scribbled inside the circle. "It says 'Lorna 2'; then these figures could be a phone number."

"That's no exchange code I know." Angus grimaced. "But we can find out." He gestured towards the two large envelopes, scattering cigarette ash in the process. "What about that stuff?"

"She was getting ready to fight a war," said Gaunt. "That looks like her ammunition. Unless you need it, I'd leave it alone."

Angus nodded. "We've enough problems—more, if she doesn't recover."

The rest of the pile thinned. They found a small, cloth-bound address book, the listings all Canadian.

"One way or another, we'll get something," Angus declared. "I'll let your people know—and we'll stay in touch with the hospital."

Gaunt nodded and glanced at his wrist-watch. "And I'll try to get home."

"I'll come down with you," said Angus. "I want to find where that young idiot Dunn has hidden himself."

They locked the door behind them when they left, then took the creaking elevator down to the hotel lobby. Angus walked with him to the main door, then stopped.

"I've got to ask this," he said awkwardly. "Is there—well, anything special about Mrs. Anderson I should know about?" He rubbed his chin and forced a grin. "I mean, I've heard you Remembrancer people are a pretty weird outfit."

"There's nothing special," Gaunt assured him. "And you've got the rest of it wrong, Sergeant. We're ordinary. The weird is what we can get landed on us."

They went out into the street. The blizzard had eased to an occasional flurry of white and the roadway had been gritted while Gaunt had been inside. He wiped the worst of the snow from the car's windscreen glass, reached for the door-handle, then saw Angus still looked unhappy.

"Something worrying you, Sergeant?" he asked.

"I don't know," said Angus slowly. "Maybe it's just the way that room was turned over—like someone was really determined." He sniffed his disgust. "Damn this weather. It's getting me down."

He went back to the hotel doorway and Gaunt got into the Ford.

As the car started and began moving, Angus gave a brief wave of farewell and went indoors.

Road conditions were still bad as Gaunt worked his way back down to Princes Street. He saw where a taxi had embedded itself in the railings on the Gardens side, close to the Scott Monument, but an ambulance was there and a policeman waved him to keep moving. He did, driving gently, following the old army winter driving code of "Keep your eyes on the road and your hoof off the brakes." Switching on the car radio, he punched buttons and located a music programme.

The route home took him close to Edinburgh Royal Infirmary. He glanced briefly at the hospital, one more bulk on the night skyline, and thought of Lorna Anderson. Her life was probably still in the balance; the thief who had raided her room was just as responsible as if he'd physically attacked her.

Even if the law wouldn't see it that way.

He reached a stretch of uncleared, ungritted road where the Ford's wheels slithered for grip. The rear-view mirror gave him a glimpse of another car in equal trouble, headlights swinging as it went into a partial skid.

Then the road took an uphill slope. Gaunt fed the car a shade more acceleration, heard the Ford's response, and avoided the temptation to do more. Children had built a snowman on some waste ground. It wore an old hat and a scarf made of sacking, and he chuckled as he passed. The snowman's face had a doleful expression that reminded him of Sergeant Angus, puzzled and wary about any involvement with the Remembrancer's Department.

Gaunt could understand it. At first, though he'd been glad to find any kind of job, he'd felt totally unsure about what it involved. On the surface, the office of Queen's and Lord Treasurer's Remembrancer appeared a total anachronism—something that could only have survived by accident.

The history side was cut and dried. The first Remembrancers had existed in mediaeval times, body servants to the early Scottish kings and queens, going around with them, literally remembering things for them, maybe even being able to read and write.

What he had discovered was that the modern Remembrancer was a senior-grade civil servant heading a department with computer-age responsibilities that spread like a thin, almost invisible web. Surviving politics, wars, reorganisations, cutbacks, generations of Remembrancers had taken on new tasks, evolved a new role, offering a home to the awkward or the unusual.

It had become quite a list.

It ran from having a say in how the law courts were run to making sure government employees didn't try to fiddle their tax returns. Sometimes involved in defence areas, the Remembrancer processed what was vaguely termed "state intelligence," handled the security of the Scottish Crown jewels, moved in on things like treasure trove, acted as a watchdog on company registrations and returns—and a whole lot more.

Including, as Lorna Anderson had discovered, *ultimus haeres*. Meaning that when anyone—even a visiting foreigner—died in Scotland without a will or heirs the Remembrancer seized everything possible for the Crown.

And no lawyer on earth had ever got round that.

Traffic lights on ahead changed to red. Letting the Ford coast towards them, Gaunt spared a glance at his rear mirror. There was only one other vehicle in sight, some distance behind him, just a pair of headlights half obscured for a moment by another flurry of snow.

He reached the traffic lights, stopped, looked again, then frowned. The other car had stopped some distance back, and there was something strangely familiar about its lights, one brighter than the other, the way a replacement unit might outperform older, original equipment.

He remembered. It was the same car he'd noticed earlier, skidding.

The lights changed. Gaunt set the Ford moving again and, curiosity roused, kept a more deliberate watch on the rear-view mirror.

The other car started again, keeping the same distance behind him.

A junction was coming up, the main route to the right, the other fork one he knew as a simple loop round some office blocks which joined the through route again. The radio was still murmuring its music and he switched it off. Then, as the junction came up, Gaunt took the left fork and kept driving at the same unhurried pace.

The car behind stayed with him, at the same distance, and was still there when he was back on the main road again.

But why? Gaunt nursed the steering-wheel with his fingertips, one part of his mind coping with keeping the car moving through the snow, the rest of his thoughts on how to find out what was going on. Then he saw a brightly lit snow-plough coming towards him through the snow flurries, followed by a long slow-moving convoy of vehicle lights.

The other car was still behind him, still keeping the same distance, and the snow-plough with its followers was coming nearer.

Dropping a gear, slamming his foot hard on the accelerator, Gaunt sent the Ford lurching forward at full throttle.

The snow-plough loomed ahead. He saw the driver's startled face as the Ford's headlights lit up the cab, saw the man's mouth shape a startled curse. Then the Ford had rammed through the snow being piled aside by the snow-plough blade and was performing a mad, barely controlled forward dance past the rest of the oncoming convoy.

He got clear and saw a narrow lane to his right. Braking, skidding, he stopped, slapped the gear lever into reverse, and took the Ford tail first into the lane's soft, deep snow. Then he stopped again, killed his lights, and waited.

The other car appeared several seconds later, fighting its way past the oncoming vehicles. It passed the lane and kept going, a big Peugeot station-wagon with two men aboard, red in colour under the street lights, registration plates obscured by snow.

Grinning, Gaunt put the Ford into gear and released the clutch, ready to reverse the roles. The little car's wheels spun furiously, but it didn't move. He tried again, and the engine stalled.

He was stuck. He got out, sank half-way up to his knees in soft snow, and saw it was hopeless.

Fifteen minutes digging with his hands got the car free. Damp and frozen, Gaunt drove the rest of the way home with the heater fan churning at full and his trouser legs gradually steaming.

Why the Peugeot had tailed him, whether it had picked him up at the hotel or later, everything about it was a mystery.

Except that it had existed and the two men aboard had been equally real.

It was 6:30 A.M. and still dark outside when the bedside clock radio came to life next morning. Gaunt had another time-switch wired to a coffee percolator and when he'd showered, shaved, and dressed, the coffee was ready to pour.

He went to the telephone, dialled the Royal Infirmary number, and got through to the hospital's inquiry desk.

"You had an emergency brought in last night, a Mrs. Lorna Anderson," he told the receptionist. "How is she?"

He had to wait. Then the girl came back on the line.

"I'm sorry." Her voice held the sympathy hospital staff kept as stock-in-trade. "Mrs. Anderson didn't regain consciousness. She died soon after midnight."

Gaunt thanked her and hung up. He poured the coffee into a mug, taking it black and without sugar, and carried the mug over to the window. The snow had stopped, the first grey traces of dawn showed a clear sky.

So Lorna Anderson hadn't made it.

He wondered how Henry Falconer would feel when he heard, and remembered Falconer's statement that the Fraser file was coming his way. Maybe Falconer could make sense out of the two men in the Peugeot.

He used the phone again to call the airport. It had reopened, with services more or less back to normal, but roads were still difficult on the way out from the city.

Finishing the coffee, Gaunt collected his coat and the black department-issue brief-case he was going to need, then left. When he reached the street, the XR3 was crusted with overnight frozen snow but still started at a touch.

The drive to the airport didn't pose too many problems, though breakdown trucks were out hauling vehicles out of ditches and other cars were still lying where they'd been abandoned. He arrived with time to spare before the Amsterdam flight was called, bought two newspapers, and checked them both.

Neither of them mentioned Lorna Anderson. Somehow, he hadn't expected they would.

Amsterdam was a hassle which lasted all day and into early evening, a low-key squabble with two Dutch government officials, a lawyer and an accountant. It centred round what was going to happen to the assets of a Dutch national who would spend the next few years in a Scottish jail for drugs offences.

The Dutch officials, both women, had him boxed in from the start. At the end, the Dutch settled for what they called a compromise and still won. When that happened they stopped being stolid and their English improved dramatically. The two women took him out to dinner and showed a formidable capacity for tankards of foam-topped beer.

His return flight was delayed. It was close on midnight before he reached Edinburgh, after 1 A.M. by the time he got home. By then, his back had begun the low-key throb which came with tiredness and Gaunt took a couple of the pain-killing tablets prescribed by the army doctors.

When he did sleep, the old, familiar nightmare soon roared in. He was falling through never-ending space, his parachute had only partially opened again. It was a nightmare which always ended just before the stark, remembered reality of impact and he jerked awake, sweating, shaking.

At last, Gaunt dozed. It was late when he wakened again and daylight had brought a thaw which had begun to turn the snow to slush. He got to the Exchequer Office in George Street at 10 A.M. and by then the gutters everywhere were flooded torrents, the pavements and roads a brown, slopping mess. Only the high-peaked roofs up above remained white.

The Remembrancer's Department, where he had his own cubbyhole of an office, was two floors up. One of the girls in the typing pool, a blonde who felt that an unmarried man was an asset going to waste, brought him coffee and a slab of cake as soon as he arrived. Then she stayed for a couple of minutes, asking about Amsterdam.

Gaunt lied a little, to brighten her day. Then, as she left, he saw a note propped against his telephone. Falconer wanted him.

He went along the corridor to the senior administrative assistant's room. Falconer's secretary, a well-built, coldly efficient woman in her thirties, pursed her lips when he arrived.

"He was looking for you almost an hour ago," she said with studied disapproval. "Since then, there's been a telex in from the Dutch. You seem to have made them very happy."

"Hannah, you always brighten my day." He grinned to annoy her. Hannah North regarded Falconer as private property, to be defended against all threats—including Falconer's wife. "Do I get my wrist slapped, or will you keep me in late after school?"

"Personally, I'd keep you in a cage." The thought pleased her. "Yes, then I'd use a long pole, with something sharp at one end."

The door to Henry Falconer's room was ajar; Gaunt tapped and went in.

"Kind of you to come," Falconer greeted him with laboured sarcasm. A big, middle-aged man with a big, middle-aged face, dressed as usual in a conservative dark suit, white shirt and golf club tie, he was standing at the window. "Damn this weather. You know that idiot tag 'the Hardy Scot'? I don't feel particularly hardy. Do you?"

"Not this morning," admitted Gaunt, closing the door. "Sorry about Amsterdam, Henry. It just didn't work out."

"You should have brought back some tulips," said Falconer. "That would have been better than nothing." He went over to the big, slow-ticking grandfather clock which adorned one corner of his office. The rest of the furniture was civil service issue but the clock was Falconer's. Opening the cabinet door, he performed his daily ritual of hauling up the weights and closed the door again. "Clever people, the Dutch—not as thick as they look. Two women?"

Gaunt nodded.

"I've heard of them. Like a Mafia hit team." Falconer left the clock, sat behind his desk, and motioned toward the chair opposite. He waited until Gaunt had settled there. "How much do you know about boats?"

"Boats?" Taken by surprise, Gaunt blinked. "Not a lot."

"That's what I expected." Falconer gave a faint shrug. "Well, it doesn't particularly matter. You know our Mrs. Anderson died?"

"Yes." Gaunt waited.

"The autopsy report says a cerebral haemorrhage; it could have happened any time." Falconer opened one of his desk drawers and brought out a bundle of papers, among them the bulky envelopes and album of old photographs Gaunt had last seen in Lorna Anderson's hotel room. Feeling the edges of the papers with his thumb,

Falconer looked anything but happy. "These make it seem she was genuine."

"Were there doubts?"

"She claimed to be related to our late Peter Fraser," said Falconer stonily. "Fraser's assets totalled over one hundred and twenty thousand pounds sterling. That buys plenty of doubt."

"But if she'd lived?"

"She had us over a barrel," admitted Falconer. "Queen's Bounty style."

It wasn't diplomatic, but Gaunt chuckled. Now and again even the Remembrancer's Department got things wrong. When that happened, when they'd already clawed in money, there was only one face-saving solution. The Queen's Bounty meant a single lump sum payment on a 'take this and go away' basis. Even if it didn't mean the Queen sitting down and writing a cheque, the civil servant who had to unlock the money-box lost a lot of popularity.

"Who handled the Fraser estate?" he asked.

"I did. There were reasons." Falconer built a steeple with his fingertips and scowled at the result.

Briefly, the only sounds were the slow ticking of the grandfather clock and an outside rumble as a mass of snow came off some roof and plunged down into George Street. Knowing George Street, Gaunt hoped it had hit one of the meter patrol traffic wardens.

"Henry." He made sure he had Falconer's full attention. "Tell me why two men with a car would want to tail me after I left Lorna Anderson's hotel on Monday night."

"Did they?" Falconer stared at him. "Do the police know?"

"Not yet." Gaunt shook his head. "But would you call it a coincidence?"

"I don't know," said Falconer wearily. "I wish I had the answers to a few things. Will I give you a start point?"

"It would help," said Gaunt.

"Our late Mr. Fraser may have had some strange friends."

"You mean he was on the crook?"

Falconer scowled. "I don't want to libel the dead."

"But you taught me they're the only ones who can't sue," said Gaunt.

"In life, he interested the police once or twice a few years ago—

suspected fraud, nothing spectacular, never charged, never convicted. In death, he left Inland Revenue's tax squad wondering how he apparently managed to escape their little skinning knives," grunted Falconer. He leaned back. "I said there was a boat—"

"You asked me if I knew about boats," corrected Gaunt.

"Same thing." Falconer treated it as irrelevant. "There's a British-registered motor yacht, the *Black Bear*, lying at a marina at Puerto Tellas, in Tenerife. The *Black Bear* was Fraser's boat—and I've had some tricky discussions with the Spanish authorities about present ownership. If the registration had been under their flag—" He shrugged. "Anyway, we've won. They agreed a few days ago, almost at the same time as the Anderson woman surfaced."

"Interesting," said Gaunt carefully. He had a sudden picture of sun and surf along a shore, a prospect ahead.

"Very." Falconer gave a nod. "The *Black Bear* is independently valued at twenty thousand pounds. There are a few final formalities to clear on the spot, then we already have an offer to purchase from one of Fraser's former associates, a resident out there."

"But someone has to go out?"

"You. The Remembrancer personally decided it was an external auditor's job; Hannah has your travel details." Until the last round of staffing cuts, Falconer had nursed his own hopes for the trip. One small, malicious consolation remained. "You're taking over the whole file, of course—not just the yacht. For instance, I've been liaising with the police over that name and telephone number in the Anderson woman's notebook."

"Lorna Two?"

"Lorna Fraser Tabor, single, lives in Winnipeg; she was in the address book you also found. I called her yesterday. Apparently another Fraser blood relation crawling out of the Canadian woodwork. She said she'd take the first available flight to Britain; in fact, I expect her here before noon."

"In full mourning?" Gaunt raised a quizzical eyebrow.

Falconer shrugged. "If she's genuine, if there aren't any more like her hidden away, she takes over from Lorna Anderson—after we've checked her out. She already knows about the Queen's Bounty situation."

"Lorna Anderson left a will," murmured Gaunt.

"It doesn't alter anything. She named this Tabor woman as her sole beneficiary." Falconer glanced at his wrist-watch, then at the grandfather clock. "I've a full schedule until she gets here, but I'll also take care of mentioning your—ah—episode with that car to the police. You can draft your final report on the Amsterdam business, then work your way through the Fraser papers—and these."

Gaunt took Lorna Anderson's bundle of documents as they were pushed across. He started to rise, but Falconer cleared his throat in a way that made him settle again.

"Anything particularly interesting in the investment world at the moment? Anything you'd call safe—my style?"

"Nothing special." He had heard a whisper of some Australian mining shares, currently cheap and chaotic, but Falconer would have had a nervous breakdown at the thought. "I could ask around."

"I had a passing thought about property." Falconer said it casually. "A small villa, or perhaps an apartment—Spain, even the Canary Islands. Property values out there usually seem to keep ahead of inflation."

"Usually," agreed Gaunt.

"Yes. Somewhere quiet, in the sun, off the beaten track." Falconer basked in the thought. "Perhaps, while you're out in Tenerife—"

"I'll ask around."

"Fraser's contacts might be able to help, if they seem reliable." Falconer beamed at him. "Fine. Hannah will give you the Fraser file —and ask her to bring in her notebook, will you?"

Gaunt left him. Outside, Falconer's secretary had the Fraser file waiting along with a ticket envelope.

"Notebook time," Gaunt told her, thumbing towards Falconer's door.

She nodded, unplugged a coffee-pot from a wall socket, and placed the pot on a tray which already held two bone china cups and saucers, sugar and cream.

"A word of warning, Jonny." The words came with a frost-edged smile. "Go easy on your Amsterdam expenses. There's a purge on this week."

Taking the tray, she headed for Falconer's door. Her shorthand notebook still lay on her desk. Falconer and Hannah always shared their coffee break and probably more.

But that was Falconer's business, and he went home at night.

He checked the ticket envelope first. There were a reservation on the next Monday scheduled flight to Tenerife from London Heathrow and a return reservation for the Thursday morning. That was probably Falconer's idea of a generous timing, but it might be enough. The *Black Bear* was lying at Puerto Tellas marina and he was to make his own arrangements when he got there.

Gaunt turned to the Amsterdam report. It took about half an hour, then he delivered the tape to the typing pool, returned, closed his office door, loosened his collar and tie, and sat down to tackle the Peter Fraser file.

It didn't take long to read and digest.

Aged forty, renting a two-roomed office in the heart of Edinburgh's business sector, Fraser had represented a Spanish-owned company named Hispan Trading, handling import, export, and general commercial contacts for firms in the Canary Islands. Fraser's office was apparently its total British representation and he ran it single-handed, only hiring occasional and casual secretarial help.

That didn't seem to have required too much effort. The Hispan office could sometimes be closed for weeks on end, then Fraser would return with a new suntan and things would pick up as before.

He lived alone in an old farmhouse cottage a few miles out of the city, near Bathgate, and the story there was the same. Every so often the cottage would lie locked and empty, then eventually his Fiat sports car would be parked outside again.

It was over a year since Peter Fraser had left his office one dark evening to drive back to his cottage. He had been almost there when the Fiat had collided head on with a delivery truck. Fraser had been killed, the truck driver had eventually been jailed for six months for reckless driving.

Peter Fraser's funeral had been attended by his lawyer, the elderly widow who cleaned his cottage, and a neighbour who drove on into Edinburgh afterwards to do some shopping. Hispan Trading sent a wreath from Tenerife.

But it ended there. Peter Fraser had no known relatives, no particular friends. His lawyer had only dealt with occasional business matters such as paying the Hispan office rental and knew nothing about a will. Hispan Trading telexed from Tenerife that Fraser had represented them for about two years and they had no knowledge of next of kin. They were installing a new manager in their Edinburgh office.

It happened. People like Fraser, people with no known background, were part of every city. When they died, there was a routine. It involved the police first, then social security and tax records, other government data banks—and legal process.

Gradually, a few facts had come together. An only child, Fraser had been born in Glasgow, the son of a Scottish shipyard worker. Fate had repeated itself: his parents had died in a car crash while he was still in his teens. No other family could be traced and he had been reared by foster-parents until he was old enough to leave them and become a merchant seaman.

There were gaps after that. A tax return mentioned two years' work in the Argentine. Later, employed briefly by a London security firm, he had broken a leg in an accident. Hospital records showed he'd answered "None" to the formal question about next of kin.

Peter Fraser had been a drifter and drifters were bad news. At last a halt was called, legal process took over, and the Queen's and Lord Treasurer's Remembrancer moved in.

The usual notices appeared in the usual newspapers. The usual letters from the usual professional claimants arrived, were investigated, dismissed.

One more announcement followed: "Notice is hereby given that the estate of the late Peter Fraser of Mallard Cottage, near Bathgate, West Lothian, has fallen to the Crown as *ultimus haeres.*"

Gaunt turned to the next page. A photograph of Fraser had been clipped to the top; taken in life, it showed a man with close-cropped hair, handsome in a thin-faced way, but with a hint of truculence about his mouth and eyes. He was wearing an open-necked shirt and the background, a dramatic coastline, had to be Tenerife.

Below it came the Remembrancer's Department final statement of executory.

Mallard Cottage had been rented by Fraser. But personal effects, including several solid gold chains, had been valued at fifteen thousand pounds. Three bank accounts added close on seventy thousand pounds; another two thousand in cash had been found in a drawer. The crashed car's replacement value, paid over by Fraser's insurance company, amounted to almost eleven thousand. Another six thousand pounds, brought together in different ways, gave a total of over one hundred thousand after allowing for funeral and other expenses. The *Black Bear* had a separate listing "at broker's valuation of twenty thousand pounds sterling."

Under the final net figure of one hundred and twenty thousand, Henry Falconer had pencilled an angry scrawl.

"Not bad on declared taxable income of sixteen thousand a year."

Gaunt grinned, skimmed the rest of the file, then turned to Lorna Anderson's papers. They had the appearance of years of work—a thick bundle of documents of all kinds, notes, old letters, even a photostat page from someone's family Bible.

Itemised where necessary in the woman's small, neat handwriting, they began in the early nineteenth century with Adam Fraser, a crofter in the parish of Glenkirk, near Inverness. Lorna Anderson had patiently charted the descendants of that long-dead Scot through generations of births, deaths, and marriages. A few of the earliest papers were yellowed, faded originals. Others were modern copy extracts and the sources, beginning in Scotland, spread to Canada and the United States, then New Zealand and the Far East and some remote corners of what had once been the British Empire.

It was all brought together in one final, carefully rolled sheet of heavy parchment paper. Lorna Anderson's idea of how to present a family tree might have made a professional genealogist cringe, but it was a tree in which every branch was detailed.

Fraser males appeared to have died in war at least as often as through accident or natural causes. Fraser females had been few and frequently childless. Branch after branch had withered.

Until only Lorna Anderson and Peter Fraser had remained, with Fraser's date of death now under his name and the note "without issue."

So where did Lorna Fraser Tabor from Winnipeg come in? Old Adam Fraser had been their common great-great-grandfather.

One of the pool typists stopped it there, coming in with a query about the Amsterdam report. As she left, one of the Companies Branch team telephoned, with an update on the case of a Dundee insurance broker who had been spending everybody's money except his own and was now dodging around the Greek islands.

"It doesn't belong with me," complained the Companies official. "What am I supposed to do with it?"

Gaunt told him.

There was a shocked silence, then the line went dead. Grinning, Gaunt hung up—and the phone immediately rang again. Sighing, he lifted it.

"Come through, Jonathan," said Henry Falconer. "Our visitor is here."

He fastened his tie as he trekked along the corridor. Hannah wasn't at her desk, and he went straight into Falconer's office. The woman sitting opposite Falconer turned in her chair as he entered and closed the door. She was in her late twenties, a brunette, wearing a grey leather jacket and trousers suit over a white roll-neck sweater. The trouser legs were tucked into neat midcalf boots; a sheepskin coat hung on Falconer's coat-rack.

"Introductions first," said Falconer, smiling. "Miss Tabor, this is Mr. Gaunt, who is handling the whole situation." He barely paused. "I've tried to save time, Jonathan: I've given Miss Tabor a basic outline of how things stand."

"As you people see it." Lorna Tabor's soft, unobtrusive Canadian accent underlined the words. She gave Gaunt a slightly weary smile. "I won't necessarily feel the same way."

"We'll try to cope," said Gaunt mildly. He looked at her for a moment, liking what he saw. She had dark eyes, high cheek-bones, and a wide, generous mouth. Her hair was cut short and her skin had a light outdoor tan, her only makeup a touch of lipstick. Apart from a wrist-watch, her only jewellery was a thin gold neck-chain worn outside the white sweater. "None of us actually met Mrs. Anderson."

"I called her Aunt Lorna—" She saw Falconer raise an eyebrow. "She asked me to do that. But I didn't know she existed until about eighteen months ago. Then she made contact, said we were—well, family, and explained how she'd traced me." She gave a faint smile. "She'd really worked at it."

Falconer nodded. "Then you kept in touch?"

"She lived in Vancouver, that's not exactly next door to Winnipeg," shrugged Lorna Tabor. "But she made the trip a few weekends and I spent a week with her last summer. I liked her."

"And if you were family, that would be enough for her," said Gaunt. He sat on the edge of Falconer's desk. "She'd talk to you about that?"

"A lot—though I'd never thought too much about where I came from." For some reason Lorna Tabor chuckled, showing perfect white teeth. "That damned family tree may have started as a hobby for Aunt Lorna, but it became the most important thing in her life." The smile ended and she turned to Falconer. "Then it killed her."

"A cerebral haemorrhage can happen any time," said Falconer uncomfortably. He glanced at the papers in front of him, then at Gaunt. "Miss Tabor intends to take care of—ah—funeral arrangements."

"Because there's no one else," said Lorna Tabor simply. "Just some distant relatives on her husband's side; that's maybe why tracing people like me mattered to her."

"The family tree," mused Gaunt. He stuck his hands in his pockets. "But your name isn't on it. Why not?"

"You could say she just wanted to pencil me in—that I was a minor embarrassment." Lorna Tabor surprised them with a chuckle, showing perfect white teeth. "Aunt Lorna was old-fashioned in some ways. My grandmother was a Fraser by birth and never married; my mother was born illegitimate, in the 1920s."

"In Canada?"

"No, here in Scotland—a family scandal. Mother and baby were packed off to Canada, double-quick, and the whole thing kept quiet. It was the way they did things then."

"That could happen," said Falconer. "The great god of Respectability. But Mrs. Anderson—?"

"Got a scent of it, followed the trail." Lorna Tabor shrugged. "My father is still alive, but my mother died about five years ago. Aunt Lorna said that now she knew about me that only left Peter Fraser in Scotland. She knew he existed, but not much more."

"Except that his line was legitimate?" suggested Gaunt. He saw

Falconer was quite happy to sit back. "You knew she was making this trip?"

"Yes."

"Thinking Fraser was still alive?"

She nodded. "Then she cabled me about a week ago, from here, saying he'd been dead more than a year, that the State had grabbed his money, but she might be able to get some of it back."

"Queen's Bounty," agreed Gaunt. "You know that you've an equal right to claim now—that your mother's illegitimacy isn't a barrier?"

"Yes." Her mouth tightened for a moment, her voice chilled several degrees. "Are you asking if that's why I'm here?"

"Some people might." Gaunt felt that it had to be said and settled. "You didn't waste any time."

Henry Falconer made a weak, protesting noise. She ignored him. Fists clenched, her dark eyes hard and angry, she got to her feet. For a moment, Gaunt thought she might hit him.

"You play rough, don't you," she said softly. "Rough and dirty—but you happen to have it wrong, Mr. Gaunt." She swung towards Falconer. "Before he came, I told you I work for a land company in Winnipeg. Maybe I should have told you my father owns the company—or would you want to see last year's balance sheet?" She drew a deep breath and glared at Gaunt again. "Yes, maybe I will claim. If I didn't I'd be a damned fool. But Lorna Anderson wanted me to come and help her. Now I'm here, I want to know exactly what the hell happened before she died."

Falconer moistened his lips. "I don't think I understand."

"Don't let it worry you," she snapped back.

"But we're paid to worry," said Gaunt. "And sometimes that means pushing people a little." He gave her an apologetic grin. "You've told us more now. How about the rest? There are things we want to find out too—and as far as I know, we're still on the same side."

Lorna Tabor didn't answer straight away. They waited the slow steady ticking of the grandfather clock seeming to dominate the room. She looked at it, walked over and considered the farming scenes painted on the old-fashioned dial. Then, at last, she sighed and turned.

"You're right—and I'm frayed, jet-lagged and the rest that goes with it." She came back to Falconer's desk. "I had a telephone call from Aunt Lorna on Sunday, from here."

Falconer stiffened. "The day before she died?"

Lorna Tabor nodded. "I was going to stay quiet about it, till I found out what was going on. But—"

"But now you'd better tell us," suggested Gaunt.

"She told me she'd found out something about Peter Fraser, something she didn't know how to handle. Then—well, she was certain she was being followed by someone."

"Followed?" Falconer swooped on the word. "Why?"

Lorna Tabor shook her head. "She said she wouldn't tell me over a phone line. But she needed me, she needed some old family papers my mother had left—and she said maybe she could make your Queen's Bounty look like peanuts."

"Did you believe her?" asked Gaunt.

"I wasn't sure." The dark-haired girl gave a small, helpless gesture. "I told her I'd have to think about it, that I couldn't just drop everything and run."

"Did she say anything else?" demanded Falconer anxiously.

"About what was going on? No. But she asked me to remember Scotch Harry."

"Who?" Falconer blinked.

"Another Fraser she kept off the family tree." Lorna Tabor grinned a little, and smoothed a hand down the edge of her leather jacket. "He was three or four generations back; he ran with Ned Kelly's wild bunch in Australia. The Australians hanged him for murder and bank robbery."

"Fascinating." Falconer swallowed hard but kept control. "You brought the papers you mentioned?"

She nodded.

"And you understand that we'll—well, still have to verify you're related to our Fraser? We'll need your help."

"When do we start?" she asked calmly.

"Now," said Gaunt. He glanced at his watch. "First we visit someone. Then we can talk some more, over lunch."

"If I stay awake long enough," she warned.

Falconer came round from his desk to help her into her coat. He shook hands with her as she left with Gaunt. Then, as the door closed and he was at last alone, the senior administrative assistant to the Queen's and Lord Treasurer's Remembrancer looked earnestly at the ceiling.

"Why me?" he asked plaintively. "Why always me?"

He flicked the intercom switch on his desk.

"Hannah," he said wearily. "Have you any aspirin out there? Bring the damned bottle!"

CHAPTER TWO

"The only other time I've been in Scotland, I was child-sized," said Lorna Tabor. "I expected all the men would wear kilts."

"And play bagpipes?" Gaunt grinned. "At that age, I thought most Canadians were lumberjacks or singing Mounties."

They were walking along Princes Street, and sunlight and slush looked like being the main ingredients to the Edinburgh scene for the rest of the day. Only the bulky mass of the castle rock was still totally covered in a mantle of white, and the shopping crowds were out again. That meant window-gazing knots of low-season tourists, bell-ringing patrols of Hare Krishna monks, and, reinforcing the local population, large, tweed-clad women in from the country trailing thin, tweed-clad men on invisible leashes.

Lorna Tabor had elected to walk and they had only a short distance to travel. She had become friendlier, and despite the tiredness in her eyes she was interested in everything around her.

"This place we're going"—she grabbed Gaunt's arm for a moment's support as they crossed another patch of slush—"you think they'll be able to help?"

"There's something wrong when they can't," he told her obliquely.

They were almost there. New Register House, at the east end of Princes Street, was an elegant dome of a neo-Georgian building mildly embarrassed by having a Woolworth's chain store as its next-door neighbour. A national repository, it treated history as just yesterday. One of its thousands of volumes of old parish records included the simple entry when Mary Queen of Scots married Darnley. Nearer the present, it held the documentation for every birth, death, and marriage in Scotland since—because the staff liked to be exact—one minute after midnight on the morning of January 1, 1855.

Anyone had access to them.

Anyone from the casual visitor to the concerned professional—and everything between, from lawyers and police to nosing journalists or suspicious wives, the occasional hopeful confidence trickster or puzzled insurance investigators.

And ancestor hunters.

A small queue of people were waiting at the main reception desk, Lorna Tabor glanced at them and frowned.

"What do we do?" she muttered. "Stand in line?"

A woman built like a duchess was arguing how much she had to pay for some photocopied extracts. She was on the staff of an Eastern Bloc consulate. The man behind her, scowling impatiently, was an Edinburgh lawyer with a reputation for charging clients as if he used a taxi-meter. The others in the queue seemed patiently resigned to waiting.

"Just smile," advised Gaunt, guiding her on. "We know people."

He knew Andy Deathstone, who had an office high up under the dome. It was a room lined with bound index volumes and with a ladder to reach the upper shelves. The only window looked inward, giving a view of the main research and reading area far below. Deathstone was small, middle-aged, and had a vague seniority in the New Register House staff.

"I knew this was going to be a bad day," he said to Gaunt. Then he eyed Lorna Tabor and smiled. "But it might get better."

Gaunt made the introductions, and Deathstone fussed to get them chairs. The little man looked as mild as a rabbit, but he and Gaunt had played poker together a few times, often enough to reveal a piranha-like side to Deathstone's actions.

"What's the problem?" asked Deathstone. Then, ignoring Gaunt again, he considered his other visitor. "Tabor—not too usual a name, but let me guess. Canada—French Canadian, probably Bois-Brûlés, somewhere around the Red River?"

"That's right." Surprised, she nodded.

"French and what?" Deathstone's interest was total. "Cree, Blackfoot?"

"Chipewyan," she corrected. She saw Gaunt was lost. "My father is a Métis—mixed blood. I work out at one-eighth Indian."

"We had a MacKenzie in from Canada last month," said Deathstone. "He's chief of a tribe in the Blackfoot Confederacy." He gestured apologetically. "That's not why you're here."

"This is." Gaunt took Lorna Anderson's handwritten family tree from his pocket, unrolled it on Deathstone's desk, and kept one hand on the paper to hold it flat. "Andy, I need this authenticated —and something extra."

Deathstone raised a quizzical eyebrow, produced a pair of thick-lensed spectacles, and studied the charted names for a moment.

"It has a reasonable feel about it," he said and glanced up. "You're going to tell me there's something missing?"

Gaunt nodded. "A birth."

"Ah." Deathstone nodded, then glanced apologetically at Lorna Tabor. "Wrong side of the blanket?"

"Yes. My mother."

"Her place of birth?"

"Inverness, Scotland, June 1924; her name was Mary Fraser, her mother was Lorna Jane Fraser."

"That's reasonably precise. Authenticating what we can of the rest may take longer—and we can't necessarily vouch for some of the overseas stuff." Deathstone paused, removed the thick-lensed spectacles, and glanced at Gaunt. "Do I ask why?"

"Would you expect much of an answer?" countered Gaunt.

"No." Deathstone was more amused than offended. "But what do you think you're holding, Jonny—a pair of tens or a full house?"

"Neither. My people are holding the pot," said Gaunt laconically. "Miss Tabor is making the call."

"Even better." Deathstone grinned. "I can enjoy this one. I take my lunch break soon; could you both come back at 3 P.M.?"

They left him. When they were in the street, Lorna Tabor looked back at the Register building with unconcealed respect.

"Is it really so easy?"

"For him, yes," said Gaunt. "People fascinate him—as long as they've been dead for a spell."

He knew a small wine bar three streets away. It was in a basement, the day's menu was chalked on a blackboard, the tables and stools were old wine barrels and cut-down casks. They found an empty table in one of the gloomier corners, ordered two glasses of the house white wine, then chose from the blackboard menu. When their drinks arrived, Lorna Tabor took a first sip from her glass, propped her elbows on the solid wood of the table, and gave a contented sigh.

"Thanks—from the last of the Frasers," she said wryly. "But stop calling me Miss Tabor. People call you Jonny, right?"

"Some do." He tasted his own drink, looking at her over the rim. She was smiling, but her eyes were tired. "Have you got an hotel room yet?"

"I'm booked in at the Carcroft—not Aunt Lorna's room, and I checked the door lock when I dropped off my suitcase." She fought back a yawn. "I asked about her things, but they said I'd need police clearance first."

"I'll try and fix it," he promised. "Anything else I can do?"

"Yes." Nursing her glass, she shaped a frown. "Jonny, once your people moved in, what happened to Peter Fraser's private stuff—personal possessions, things like that?"

"They'd be sorted out, mostly sold at a public auction or destroyed."

"But not the yacht at Tenerife." She smiled at his surprise. "Your Mr. Falconer sort of mentioned it, and that you were going out there."

"At the end of the week."

"To sell." She nodded her understanding. "All right. I won't challenge that. But I think I'll do what Falconer suggested and get myself a lawyer. Now—how about telling me about Peter Fraser?"

"There's not a lot." He paused as the waiter arrived with the bowls of soup and the toasted sandwiches they'd ordered. "What did Falconer say?"

"Very little. He was too busy trying to find out about me."

Gaunt chuckled. Then, while they ate, he quietly sketched through most of what he knew. When he'd finished, he knew the young, dark-haired woman sitting so close to him was disappointed.

"It's not enough," she said. "Look, Jonny, Lorna Anderson was only here about three weeks. She found out something; how?"

He shook his head. "I wish I knew."

"Then that hotel robbery—could it have been for a reason?"

He shrugged. "Maybe."

"Maybe gets a hell of a lot of use around here," she said caustically. Then, just as quickly, she sighed. "I'm sorry, but I can't forget how she sounded when she made that last telephone call. She was scared, Jonny. Whatever she'd discovered, she was scared."

"I'm ready to believe that," he said quietly. Their glasses were empty. He signalled the waiter to bring two more.

"Then what do we do?"

"We?"

"Yes." She made it a challenge, then waited, taking a pack of cigarettes from her purse and lighting one.

"You've got enough to do for now," he said slowly. "But I can try to find out more about where she went—and get more background on Peter Fraser."

For a moment she seemed ready to argue. Then, reluctantly, she nodded.

A little later, Gaunt paid the bill. His back had stiffened again, and he winced as he rose to help Lorna Tabor with her sheepskin coat.

"Something wrong?" she asked.

"Rust," he said wryly. "Blame the weather; there's a lot of it about."

"I've noticed." She looked at him for a moment but said nothing more.

It was still early. Gaunt had heard the thud of the one o'clock time gun firing from the castle while they'd been eating; most of the city was still on its lunch-break.

Lorna Tabor didn't object when he suggested she take the chance and go back to the Carcroft to unpack. She stood stifling another yawn while he hailed a taxi for her.

"I'll meet you at New Register House at three," promised Gaunt as they parted. "If I'm late, ask for Andy Deathstone."

As her taxi pulled away, he started walking to where his Ford was parked. He got aboard, sat behind the wheel for a moment, then made up his mind and set the car moving.

Central Division police station was hidden up a side street off Leith Walk. He got there at the same time as a large, struggling drunk was brought in by a couple of policewomen. The drunk wanted to charge the policewomen with assault and was walking as if it still hurt. Gaunt waited until the noise had cleared from the general office then asked for Detective Sergeant Angus.

Angus was in. He came along a corridor to find Gaunt reading the wanted posters on the station notice-board.

"You." The horse-faced detective didn't pretend to be pleased. "What's it this time?"

"Can we talk?" asked Gaunt.

Angus beckoned and led the way through to the main C.I.D. room. For the moment, they had it to themselves. Angus's desk was beside a radiator. He had a carton of milk and a sandwich lying to one side of the typewriter he'd been using. He dragged over another chair for Gaunt, then slumped into his own.

"I've got to go out in a few minutes." He swallowed some of the milk. "Crime Prevention conned me into giving a talk to a school class. Half the kids there probably know more about crime than I do. So—?"

"Lorna Anderson," said Gaunt. "How do things stand?"

"They don't," said Angus gloomily, taking a bite from his sandwich. He chewed for a moment. "Scenes of Crime drew a blank in her room—not as much as a smudged fingerprint. We circulated a list of the junk she said was stolen, but none of it has turned up." He shrugged. "We've nothing else."

"But you had doubts," reminded Gaunt.

"Yes." Angus showed his yellowed teeth in a grimace. "And you were followed—but we only hear about it today."

They considered each other in silence. At last, Angus gestured towards his typewriter.

"Like to guess how many reports I've had to write because that woman died?"

Gaunt shook his head. "Only if any of them mention Peter Fraser."

"He's mentioned." Angus took more of his sandwich and another swallow of milk. "I got curious about him afterwards and asked around."

"And?" Gaunt raised a hopeful eyebrow.

"I don't think he ran much risk of being asked to join a Rotary Club." The detective grinned. "Though who knows, these days? The Fraud Squad had him on their books a few times, but never did nail him for anything. That was his style: they had him tabbed as a good front man in some low-risk confidence tricks, the kind that don't often backfire. But he dropped out of the frame two, maybe three, years back."

"Would that be when he got the Hispan job?"

Angus nodded.

"Did anyone take a look at Hispan?"

"They're foreign but they seem legitimate enough." Angus made it clear that, as far as he was concerned, the two things together were unusual. "No complaints from anyone, and they don't do a lot of business." He got on with his lunch again. "Anything else?"

"We've a relative of Lorna Anderson's in town now—from Canada. She wants to know about Mrs. Anderson's property."

"It's here," nodded Angus. "If she's authorised, we'll be glad to get rid of it."

"But I want to see it first," said Gaunt.

Angus sighed, lumbered to his feet, and led the way.

The division's regular property and productions room was being painted and two spare cells were being used. Going into one of them, Angus located a suitcase and a plastic sack, dumped both on a small table, and stood back.

"That's everything." Noise was filtering through to them from farther down the cell block. Gaunt recognised the voice: the drunk he'd seen brought in now claimed he needed a doctor. Angus ignored the shouts. "Look, can I leave you on your own? That's not going by the rule book, but I've got these damned kids—"

"If I want to borrow anything, I'll ask first," promised Gaunt.

"Fine." The detective hesitated. "About Fraser—was he on the crook when he died?"

"It's possible," said Gaunt. "If that does surface, I'll let you know."

Angus left him. In the background, the drunk farther along the cell block had fallen silent, giving up.

Gaunt turned to the case and plastic sack. The case, the one with the slashed lid he'd seen at the hotel, had been neatly packed by someone. The plastic sack had a hospital tag and apparently held the clothes Lorna Anderson had been wearing when she arrived there by ambulance. The fact she was dead now didn't make what he had to do any easier.

The suitcase yielded nothing new. He turned to the hospital sack and spread its contents over the table. A quilted blue parka, trimmed with grey fur, had two outside pockets. One was empty, the other held a handkerchief and the remains of a bar of chocolate. He was folding the parka again, ready to put it back in the sack, when he spotted an inside pocket. Checking it, he thought it was empty at first. Then his fingers met crumpled paper.

The pocket had a hole at the foot; most of his find had slipped through into the lining. Gaunt teased the single sheet out and flattened it on the table.

Headed "Hispan Properties," it was an advertising leaflet offering properties for sale in the Canary Islands. At the foot were two boxes giving Hispan's addresses in Edinburgh and Tenerife. Full-colour illustrations showed villas and apartment blocks with a foreground of bronzed girls in bikinis and a backdrop of swimming-pools and palm trees. Hard-sell advertising copy talked of sun, sea, and warm, romantic nights.

He grinned and turned the leaflet over. The reverse side listed purchase prices and finance plans without mentioning possible interest rates. But a whole series of pencilled figures ran down one of the margins, all in Lorna Anderson's small, neat handwriting. He looked at them and stopped grinning.

First there was a telephone number, meticulously circled. Then a small series of calculations, converting British pounds into dollars, were followed by another circled telephone number. The sums involved in the calculations were modest; both telephone numbers began with local Edinburgh exchanges.

The drunk in the cell along the way came to life again, singing off key, slurring his words, happy now. Another prisoner began shouting, telling him to shut up. Ignoring the noise, Gaunt repacked the rest of the clothing. Then, with a silent apology to Sergeant Angus, he slipped the leaflet into an inside pocket and left.

The officer on duty at the general office said Angus had gone out. Gaunt asked if he could use a telephone, and one was pushed across.

He dialled the first of the telephone numbers and it rang out, then was answered.

"Universal Travel," said a voice. "Can we help you?"

Mouth tightening, he broke the connection and dialled the second number. This time, a woman's voice answered.

"Good afternoon," she said briskly. "Spanish Consulate."

He hung up and swore under his breath.

"No luck?" asked the hovering duty officer.

"Not a lot," said Gaunt.

But he wondered. If Lorna Anderson had been thinking of travel, if Tenerife had been her possible destination, he didn't think the Canadian widow's reasons had had anything to do with property investment.

He thanked the constable, then went out to his car. One thing was certain. It was time to find out a little more about Hispan Trading, even if that meant being late for the meeting with Andy Deathstone.

Hispan Trading's office was in Calvin House, a large glass-and-concrete commercial development located on the edge of a strip of green parkland Edinburgh called the Meadows. Calvin House was owned by an absentee landlord insurance company; the first two floors were occupied by a computer sales organisation, and the other floors housed a variety of tenants.

There was a directory board in the lobby. Jonathan Gaunt was standing checking it when a small, wizened man in a grey porter's uniform came over.

"Lost?" he asked.

"Where's Hispan Trading?" asked Gaunt.

"Them?" The little man gave a monkey-like grin. "Fourth floor. But I haven't seen any of them today, except young Angela. Don't particularly expect to, either."

"They seem difficult to contact," said Gaunt.

"Difficult?" The little man snorted. "Do you know them?"

"No." Gaunt shaped a grimace. "That's my problem."

The little man gave him a wise look. "What's your line? Selling?"

"Well—" Gaunt left it at that.

"I'll give you a tip." The little man lowered his voice confidentially. "The boss is a tall, thin character, John Cass. Looks soft, talks the same way. But don't let that fool you. He can be a hard man if things don't go right."

He winked and ambled away.

Gaunt took the elevator up to the fourth floor. Hispan Trading's office was the last door on the left, past a trade union branch and a photographic agency. He went in, and a chubby-faced girl looked up from her desk, then put down the magazine she'd been reading. Her desk was the main piece of furniture in the sparsely furnished room.

"Hello." She eyed Gaunt with open curiosity.

"Hello." He smiled at her. "Is John Cass in?"

"No. Just me." She was about twenty, with mousey hair, a button nose, a multicoloured sweater and an air of total boredom. "I'm Angela."

Gaunt nodded. "The porter told me."

"Charlie?" She grinned. "He's the resident gossip."

He looked around. There were two filing cabinets beside her desk and a couch and small table near the window. Some photographs of villas and apartments were pinned onto the walls and a closed door behind the girl was marked "Private."

"Suppose I want to buy an apartment?" he asked.

"I take the inquiries, then pass them on." The girl chewed a fingernail for a moment. "Mr. Church is the property salesman, but he's part time, usually works from home. I could give you some leaflets—"

"No thanks." Gaunt tried again. "When will John Cass be in?"

"I'm not sure," she said vaguely. "He phoned this morning and said he might be here late this afternoon. Mr. Cass only looks in now and again; sometimes I see him, sometimes I don't. I just look after the office and answer the phone."

Gaunt nodded sympathetically. "How long have you worked for Hispan?"

"About two months." She inspected the fingernail she'd been chewing and seemed satisfied. "It's just temporary."

"And dull?"

"There's not much to do," she admitted.

"Someone I knew came here not long ago," said Gaunt casually. "A Canadian woman, in her sixties. Remember her?"

"Mrs. Anderson?" The girl grinned. "Yes. She kept phoning and calling until she got hold of Mr. Cass. Then she came here and they had a talk."

"When?"

"About a week ago." She leaned her elbows on the desk, obviously glad of an audience. "I don't know what happened, Mr.—uh—"

"Gaunt."

"Well, they were in Mr. Cass's office. And he wasn't too happy after she left."

"Did they have a row?"

The girl frowned. "No, I don't think so. I mean, I didn't hear any shouting. But he was angry about something; then he told me to take the rest of the afternoon off." She stopped. "Should I be telling you all this?"

"No." He smiled at her. "But don't let it worry you, Angela. I'll maybe look in again."

She nodded, and picked up her magazine as he went out. When he reached the lobby, the little porter waved a casual farewell.

It wasn't easy to find a parking space around New Register House. Finally, he managed to slide the Ford into a newly vacated slot, then splashed through the last of the Princes Street slush and went into the building.

When he got there, Lorna Tabor was already in Andy Death-stone's office. They sat side by side, their heads bent over a scatter of documents spread on a table in front of them.

"Where the hell have you been?" asked Deathstone, removing his thick-lensed spectacles. He scowled. "I sweat blood to do you a favour, and what do you do?"

"Turn up late," said Gaunt apologetically. He pulled over a chair, sat opposite them, and glanced at Lorna. "How has he made out?"

"It's amazing." She gestured at the spread of documents in near-disbelief. "Everything's here. Names, places, dates—"

"And the Canadian papers Miss Tabor has complete it, Jonny," said Deathstone, equally pleased. "As far as I'm concerned, she's Grade A approved, a direct descendant of Adam Fraser, crofter."

"Last sprig on the family tree?"

"We can't find any other."

"He'll want that in writing," Lorna warned. "Probably in triplicate."

"No problem." The small, middle-aged figure beamed. "That family tree of Mrs. Anderson's was excellent—amateurish but excellent. Then, of course, I've explained to Miss Tabor that tracing descendants is usually a damned sight easier than going for ancestors." He sighed at the thought. "People come in here and say they want to know about their ancestors. Damn it, go back six generations and everybody can claim sixty-four great-great-great-great-grandparents—"

"I'll take your word for it," said Gaunt hurriedly. He smiled at Lorna. "If Andy says you're legal, even Henry Falconer will go along with it."

"So now everybody agrees I exist." Her quiet Canadian drawl didn't hide the sarcasm behind the words. "Good."

"I traced my wife's family tree once," mused Deathstone. "Then she wished I hadn't. I discovered a couple of particularly nasty skeletons in her ancestral cupboard, nice conversation stoppers." He sat back and folded his arms. "Jonny, I've got to ask you this. What the heck has been going on?"

"Meaning what?" Gaunt raised an eyebrow.

"Meaning our records staff are getting slightly sick of the name Fraser," said Deathstone almost peevishly. "First, we had requests soon after he died. Then—well, this is the third in the last couple of weeks. One was Lorna Anderson." He paused and glanced at Lorna. "That's a clue on its own, of course. 'Lorna' is a regular name in your family." He saw Gaunt's impatience and cleared his throat. "Yes—first Lorna Anderson, about two weeks ago. Then, a few days later there was a man."

"Did he have a name?" demanded Gaunt.

Deathstone sighed. "Yes. At least, he signed the request slips as John Smith."

"That helps," said Gaunt drily.

"These are public records," said Deathstone defensively. "We don't ask for reasons or identification."

"Any way he could come across a mention of a Lorna Tabor?"

"No." Deathstone was positive. "Lorna Tabor only exists in Canada."

"Do your people remember anything about John Smith?"

"No." Deathstone shook his head sadly. "Sorry."

Lorna Tabor frowned at each of them, puzzled.

"Would one of you like to explain what the hell you've been talking about?" she asked.

"Peter Fraser, your Aunt Lorna, and someone who became interested in them both," said Gaunt quietly. "There was the break-in at her room, then other things. Add them together, remember what she told you."

"Like how she hinted Peter Fraser was a crook?" Lorna nodded.

Gaunt saw Andy Deathstone was listening, bewildered. But that wasn't important.

"Maybe there is this hidden money or something else that matters," he said slowly. "And it looks like someone else wants to get to it first."

She sat silent for a moment, still looking at him, a stray ray of sunlight from the window glinting on her dark hair. Her face, suddenly empty of emotion, could have been an Indian carving in stone. But her dark eyes were angry.

"He won't," she said simply. "Not if I can damned well help it. I owe her that much."

Andy Deathstone gave Gaunt a slight headshake, meaning explanations could wait but he'd want them later. They thanked him and left.

A tour bus was unloading its well-wrapped, camera-hung passengers outside the building. Their guide was gathering them into a group, like so many sheep, counting heads.

"Jonny." Lorna touched Gaunt's arm as they went past the group. "Can you spare me some time?"

He nodded. "That's why I'm here."

"Then"—she hesitated—"then would you show me where Peter Fraser is buried?"

He tried to hide his surprise. But there had been a note in the department file, along with a statement of funeral costs.

"Yes. Why?"

"I'm not sure," she admitted. "I just feel I should—well, know." She gave a wry twist of a smile. "Humour me, will you?"

Gaunt nodded and led her to where he'd left the Ford.

The cemetery was on the southeast side of the capital, big and old, a stark, desolate place in the winter sunlight. Leafless trees stood like gaunt mourners, the last of the melting snow still dripping from their branches onto mildewed gravestones. Vandals had broken the head from a winged angel guarding a tomb near the entrance and had spray-painted a couple more nearby.

Gaunt stopped his car at the cemetery superintendent's office and went in. The superintendent, a bald, elderly man, abandoned a cup of coffee and a blazing coal fire when he saw he had a visitor.

"No problem." He nodded cheerfully when Gaunt asked where Fraser's grave was located. "Are you a relative?"

"Distant," lied Gaunt.

"Right." The man went over to a cupboard, hummed under his breath while he consulted a ledger, then came back. "It's in one of the new sections. Take the third avenue on the right, straight along till you come to the Fergus family; it's a damned great monument like the Taj Mahal gone wrong. Take the left-hand path from there."

Gaunt thanked him and turned to go.

"The ground's a bit slippery down there," warned the superintendent. "Mud. Can't keep things tidy this time of year." He grinned. "Not that we get many complaints."

Lorna was standing beside the car when Gaunt returned. They walked together between the close lines of graves, reached the Fergus memorial stone, then went along a narrow gravel-covered path.

The "new section" was no pleasant place. They passed two newly dug, waiting graves topped by planks and canvas. Others were still low humps of settling, broken earth. Mud and small patches of snow seemed everywhere.

Peter Fraser's plot was a comparative oasis of uncut grass with a simple headstone. His name and the date of his death were on the stone in leaded black lettering.

Gaunt glanced at Lorna. She gave him a small, reassuring smile, took a step nearer, then stopped and frowned.

A withered wreath of flowers lay on the grass at the base of the stone. Stooping, Gaunt lifted it and disturbed a large white slug in the process. A small card, almost reduced to pulp, was still attached to the wreath by thin green twine. But the smudged message it bore was still readable.

"What does it say?" Lorna came beside him and read the words aloud, softly. " 'Remembering. Marta, Puerto Tellas.' That's Tenerife?"

He nodded. "And where his boat is lying."

"Marta." She said the name thoughtfully. "A woman; you're sure he hadn't anyone out there?"

"If you mean a wife, no. We checked." Gaunt broke off the card, put it in a pocket, and returned the withered wreath to the wet grass. "Want to—well, stay for a moment?"

"No." She shook her head. "I've been. That's enough."

They went back to the car, then Gaunt on his own made another visit to the superintendent's office.

"Find him all right?" asked the man, not bothering to stir from the warmth of his coal fire.

Gaunt nodded. "There was a wreath. Has anyone else been asking about the grave?"

"Fraser?" The cemetery superintendent scratched his chin. "No, he hasn't had visitors. But I remember the wreath. We don't get too many that way."

"What way?"

"Delivered." The man shrugged. "This florist's van arrived. The driver had the wreath with him, said it had been sent Interflora. You know, ordered by cable."

"Can you remember the firm's name?"

"No. But I know when. It was the first anniversary of his death—spot on." The superintendent gave a soft chuckle. "There's always someone, somewhere, eh?"

"Somewhere," agreed Gaunt.

Dusk comes early to Scotland in winter and the sky was already grey as they drove back into the city. By the time they stopped outside the Carcroft Hotel the first street lights were coming to life.

"Enough for one day?" Gaunt asked.

"The way I feel, yes." Lorna Tabor, her door half opened, rested back against the seat for a moment. She looked tired. "A bed and some sleep, that's most of my programme—a bed and a lot of sleep, just as soon as I've phoned my father in Winnipeg."

"About tomorrow," said Gaunt. "Henry Falconer will want to see you again."

"Now I'm legal?" She shrugged. "I'll think about it. I've a few things to sort out."

"Tell me," invited Gaunt.

"Later." She managed to stifle a yawn. "I want to do some thinking first, Jonny. Maybe talk to some people, get some advice." Her lips pursed for a moment. "Will you help me do one thing?"

"Tomorrow?" He nodded. "If it's legal."

"Before she left Canada, Aunt Lorna wrote to various places and got hold of an old address for Peter Fraser. My guess is she'd work on from there. Then, when she found he was dead—well, at least she'd know about the cottage where he'd been living. I'd like to see it."

Gaunt nodded. "I can probably arrange that. In fact, I'll come with you."

"I was counting on that. Thanks." She smiled at him and got out of the car.

Gaunt waited until she'd gone into the hotel, then set the Ford moving again. He had a choice between seeing Henry Falconer or trying the Hispan Trading office again, and he'd had enough of Falconer for one day.

There was more traffic on the roads, the build-up towards the evening rush-hour, and when he reached Calvin House there was already a choice of empty parking places.

Gaunt took the elevator up to the fourth floor. Hispan Trading's outer office was in semidarkness and deserted, but a light showed behind the frosted glass of the private office at the rear. He could hear a murmur of voices, indistinct but belonging to two men. Going over, he knocked on the door, and the voices stopped. He heard the scrape of a chair being shoved back, and a moment later the door swung open.

"How the hell did you get in?" asked a tall, thin man.

Gaunt thumbed towards the main door. "It wasn't locked."

"Damn that girl." The man, about Gaunt's age, had close-cut fair hair, a small mouth, and a large beak of a nose. His voice was soft, just short of being a woman's, and he wore a grey business suit with a white shirt and wine-coloured silk tie. He stayed where he was, blocking the view into the private office. "We're closed. Come back tomorrow."

"If you happen to be John Cass, this will only take a minute," said Gaunt easily.

The man frowned, but nodded. "Well?"

"I was here earlier." Gaunt showed his Remembrancer's identification. "I told Angela I'd be back."

"She mentioned someone had been." Cass's small mouth tightened a little. "You asked about the Canadian woman. Why?"

"She died," said Gaunt.

Cass shrugged. "I didn't know."

"No reason you should," said Gaunt. "But there's a legal problem. It goes back to Peter Fraser."

"I thought it might." Cass glanced deliberately at his wrist-watch. It was gold, with a thick, matching bracelet. "I'm in the middle of a private meeting, but I'll give you two minutes, no more."

Gaunt nodded. Cass came out into the main office, carefully closing the door behind him.

"Mrs. Anderson happened to be a distant relation—" began Gaunt.

"I got all that the first time I met her," said Cass wearily. "The family tree waved under my nose, the lot."

"Then how often did you see her?"

"Twice, which was twice too often," snapped Cass. "She badgered her way in, the first time about two weeks ago, then last week —last Wednesday."

"What did she want?"

Cass's thin shoulders shaped a shrug. "The woman seemed to think we might have some of Fraser's stuff still lying around."

"And did you?"

"No." Cass made it plain he was trying to be patient. "Look, I never knew Fraser. I came here after his death; one of the first things I had to cope with was his lawyer and the police wanting to go through his desk." He pursed his lips. "They took a few things. Anything they left behind was thrown out—anything, everything."

"You told Lorna Anderson?"

"Twice. Maybe she thought we had a bag of gold hidden away." Cass rubbed a finger down one side of his beak of a nose and sniffed derisively at the thought. "So what's happened now? You say she's dead. Has another like her turned up?"

"There's a possibility," said Gaunt vaguely. "And we haven't totally settled Fraser's estate."

"That yacht." The thin man sniffed again. "I was talking to head office in Tenerife yesterday. They mentioned someone was going out to Puerto Tellas to sell the thing. You?"

Gaunt nodded.

"Then you'll meet my boss, Paul Weber. Ask him about Fraser; he knew him well enough."

"Will Marta be there?" asked Gaunt mildly.

"Weber's sister?" Cass stopped and blinked. "I suppose so. How does she come into it?"

"Someone mentioned her," said Gaunt vaguely. "What's she like?"

"Like the boss's sister," countered Cass. "Finished?"

"For now, yes." Gaunt ambled over to one of the displays of property posters. "I've a friend making noises about buying one of your apartments. How's the market?"

"Reasonable." Cass hesitated then added grudgingly. "Tell him to contact us. Or you could have a word with Paul Weber when you're out: he's building a development at Puerto Tellas as a sideline."

Cass shepherded him towards the main door and out into the corridor. The door closed again, and he heard the click of a lock. John Cass was making sure there would be no further interruption.

Gaunt walked to the elevator, pressed the call-button, and thought while he waited. At least the name Marta now meant something. But Cass hadn't asked how Lorna Anderson had died.

Either he didn't care or, despite what he'd said, he knew.

The elevator arrived. Gaunt squeezed in beside a chattering group of secretaries and they fell silent, looking him up and down, leaving him feeling like a bull in a sale ring.

He let them leave first when the elevator reached the lobby. Then, as he headed out of the building, Charlie the hall porter appeared in his path.

"Back again?" the wizened little man in grey uniform gave him a grin. "Any luck this time? I saw Cass in the building."

"We had a talk." Gaunt stopped, remembering the porter was Calvin House's resident gossip. "But he kept it short; he had someone with him.

"Probably one o' that bunch he calls 'business associates.' " The little porter gave a dry cackle of a laugh. "I wouldn't like to meet any o' them on a dark night."

Another wave of homebound office-workers came heading for the door. Gaunt took him by the arm and eased him to one side, next to a concrete tub filled with greenery.

"You could help me, Charlie," he said quietly. "Angela said you'd a pretty good memory. Do you remember Peter Fraser?"

"The one who died?" The porter rubbed his chin. "I might, friend. But my throat can get dry."

"Would this help?" Gaunt produced two pound notes, folded them, and waited.

"I think so." Charlie expertly palmed the notes. "Fraser had the same visitors, right?"

"I've heard he wasn't around very much."

"Away more than half o' the time, and his mail piling up; it's still the same." The porter scowled. "We've got some weird tenants in this place, but that Hispan outfit win hands down."

"How much mail does Hispan get?"

"Plenty of books an' magazines—which must cost them. But not much in the way o' letters." Absent-mindedly, the little porter stripped some leaves from the nearest plant and crumpled them in one hand. "Mail—I heard enough about it when that long beanpole up there took over."

Gaunt frowned. "Trouble?"

"Aye. He'd hardly got here before he started shouting. First he said there were office files missing and wanted to know if the cleaners had thrown anything out."

"Had they?"

"If it's in a waste bucket, it gets heaved; that's all. But then he started blaming me for losing mail he said should have come."

"And?"

"I just told him to go to hell," said the little man proudly.

"You said books and magazines," reminded Gaunt casually. "The interesting kind?"

"No. Business stuff, technical things. The nearest thing to a pin-up in any o' them would be a five-ton truck," said the porter caustically. "They came—they still come—then most of them are thrown out unopened. That's more work for the cleaners, an' more work for me."

"It's a hard world," murmured Gaunt.

"A damn thirsty one too, eh?" The little man gave him a gnomish wink. "Any time you want another wee chat about things, look in."

"Any time I can afford it, I will," promised Gaunt. "Goodnight, Charlie."

Edinburgh's nightly emptying ritual was near its peak. By the time Jonathan Gaunt got back to the Exchequer Building, the Remembrancer's Department was almost deserted.

For twenty minutes he sat at one of the typewriters in the otherwise empty typing pool area and tapped out a basic, outline report for Henry Falconer. Finished, he corrected some of the more blatant typing errors in ink, put the report in an envelope, and dropped it in the internal mailbox.

Then he left.

It was Wednesday, and Wednesday night was poker night. He was one of half a dozen regulars in a tightly knit "school," and the rules were simple. The game rotated to a different house each week, the stakes weren't allowed to cause financial disaster.

It was the turn of John Milton to play host. Milton was a stockbroker with enough humour to have the telegraphic address Paradise Lost and enough patience to cope with Gaunt's investment whims.

He also had a wife who spent Wednesday evenings at keep-fit classes.

John Milton lived in a big old house in the Barnton area, where most of his neighbors were other stockbrokers, company directors, or retired generals. On the way over, Gaunt stopped at a restaurant for a sandwich and it was about eight when he parked his car behind the other vehicles already outside the house.

He crunched up a gravel path, through a tree-lined garden which looked like a neglected public park, and rang the doorbell; after a few moments a porch light snapped on. Then the door opened.

"We've started," said Milton, beckoning him in. "You're late."

"I was working," said Gaunt.

"That brings tears to my eyes," said Milton and led the way through to his study.

He was last to arrive, and a hand was in progress. The dealer, a trade union official, greeted him with a wink. The other regulars included a geriatrician, a right-wing city councillor, and a professional footballer. But one of the players was Andy Deathstone.

Gaunt waited. The hand finished and Deathstone ambled over to join him.

"I hoped you'd show up," said Deathstone amiably. "That's why I came over tonight."

Gaunt nodded, and they stood for a moment, watching the new hand being dealt.

"Like to tell me what this Fraser business is all about?" asked Deathstone as the cards were lifted. He settled his small, plump shape against Milton's desk. "When people start playing fast and loose with New Register House I prefer to know why."

"Money," said Gaunt, his eyes on the game. Milton, with four queens, was being bluffed superbly by the geriatrician, who nursed three tens. "Probably a lot of money—if it exists."

"And your Miss Tabor had to prove she exists." Deathstone nodded. "I checked around again after you left, Jonny. Your Mrs. Anderson—the late Mrs. Anderson—kept our staff busy. Not just your basic family tree stuff; she wanted reference books, then some of the old parish records, and even tried nibbling at some of the overseas archival stuff in the other records sections."

"Did she say why?"

"Vague noises, and we don't push it," reminded Deathstone. "But she used us like we were a lending library."

Milton scowled round at them from the table and told them to shut up.

"What could she get from the overseas side?" murmured Gaunt after a moment.

"Just about anything. Though our people had a feeling she was maybe disappointed." Deathstone gestured expansively. "The trouble is, there's so much lying around. You get a family clearing out after someone dies, and they find an old shoe-box of diaries, letters left over from when Granddad tried to make his fortune abroad.

They dump them on us. You want to know what North America was really like before those uppity colonials forgot their manners? We can give you chapter and verse. Or if you want India under the Raj, maybe Africa whilst Livingstone was doing his tourist bit—"

A concerted growl from the poker game stopped him there.

They joined the game at the next hand. Gaunt pushed his luck with two high pairs and was hammered by John Milton with a fat hearts-and-diamonds flush.

"That's what happens when you don't pay attention," said Milton, scooping up the pot. "Whose deal?"

As usual, the game ended at midnight. Nobody had lost much, nobody had won much. One by one, the players said goodnight and left, but Gaunt hung back, finishing a can of beer, watching Milton slotting a pile of plastic chips into their storage box.

"John, give me a help with something," he said as Milton finished. "Suppose I want to hide away money, hide it so the tax man doesn't sniff it. I know where he might look, so what do I do?"

"How about a tin box under your bed?" Milton grinned. "Since when did you have that kind of worry?"

"I think someone did. Then he died."

"And we presume he didn't take it with him." Milton sighed, opened a can of beer for himself, and took a gulp. "Dirty money?"

Gaunt nodded.

"Then its a laundry job." Milton wiped a hand across his mouth. "Swiss banks are fussier than they used to be. There's the Caribbean; I know places where they'll let you set up your own bank if you want."

"How about Spain?"

"Tricky. Not impossible, but tricky." Milton shook his head.

"And here, in Britain?"

"There's always 'Now you see it, now you don't.' " Milton took another sip from his can. "It's like playing snakes and ladders. You use different banks, different names, different accounts. The money moves around, back and forward, in small lots, fast. Except you're always draining some off to where you really want it."

"Somewhere different?"

Milton nodded. "You've bought yourself a little private company, ceased trading, more or less dormant, assets just about zero. You keep reversing money into it—simple, no fuss. The company isn't trading, so you don't have to make tax returns."

"It happens?"

"Some of my best friends deny it," said Milton, and grinned.

A chill, gusting wind from the northeast was rustling its way through the trees and shrubbery as Gaunt left Milton's house and began walking back through the garden towards his car.

He heard the sound of breaking glass as he reached a thick patch of laurel beside the entrance gate. He ran forward, then swore.

A burly figure wearing a heavy parka jacket stood at the front of his Ford. One headlamp had just been smashed in, the man was already swinging a short metal bar of some kind, aiming a blow at the other light.

Gaunt shouted and began sprinting. The second headlamp glass shattered then the man turned, grinning.

And a second figure slipped out of the shadows.

Gaunt stopped, watching them come towards him. The second figure, parka-clad like his companion, was swinging a bottle as they closed in. Neither said a word.

He had to let it happen, had to let them come close in. That had been the gospel according to a gritty little unarmed-combat instructor in the Parachute Regiment who made life hell if you got it wrong and slightly worse if you got it right. Don't think it: do it. And do it first.

They were almost on him when he moved. A roar of simulated, bubbling rage, a rush forward, a sideways blow at the one who had smashed the headlamps. Then Gaunt concentrated briefly on the thug with the bottle.

He dodged a wild swing and aimed for his head, and it grazed his shoulder. He countered hard and fast, kicking the thin figure just below the left knee. Screaming with pain, the man lurched back and the bottle smashed as it was dropped.

Snarling, the second thug came in. His iron bar lashed the air like a whip, he was ready for Gaunt to retreat. That left him unprepared for the opposite as his target used footwork again, fast sideways and forward. Almost behind the man, Gaunt grabbed his arm, jerked him round, then butted him hard and square on the face.

Half stunned, lips smashed, nose pouring blood, the parka-clad attacker staggered blindly. Then, suddenly, headlights were coming towards them.

One man cried a warning. Both fled at a shambling run.

As the car arrived and braked to a halt, John Milton came hurrying down the gravel path from his house. He was armed with a golf club.

"I heard noises," he began. "What the hell's going on?"

The car driver, a middle-aged women, climbed out.

"I saw them," she snapped angrily. "Drunks—this whole damned area is going to pieces. And do you want to know what our overpaid police are doing about it?" She gestured angrily in towards the city. "A whole damned carload are back there, running a speed trap."

Tight-lipped, Milton looked at the Ford then at Gaunt.

"You all right?" he asked.

Gaunt nodded.

"Good." Milton frowned at a stain on the roadway. "That's blood. Yours?"

"No."

"Even better."

"What's wrong with flogging anyway?" asked the woman driver to the world in general.

"Drunks." Milton looked at him again, faintly suspicious. "Do I call the police?"

Gaunt shook his head. Both men would be far away by now. He wondered how many drunks ended up wandering an exclusive area like Barnton, or would have chosen his car as their target.

He thanked Milton and the woman, then got into his car. It started as usual. Though the headlamp glasses had been smashed, both bulbs still worked.

And it was time to drive home.

CHAPTER THREE

He was late for work again next morning.

Leaving the little black Ford at Dan Cafflin's repair shop, its two smashed headlamps like reproachful wounds, was almost as bad as consigning a relative to a hospital ward.

Maybe worse, when he thought of the few relatives he had around.

Cafflin's workshop was a grimy hut on the edge of an Edinburgh canal, surrounded by dilapidated tenement property. Cafflin, a large hulk of a man, frowned at the damage, picked up an oil-stained note-pad, and scribbled quickly with a stub of pencil. He showed the result to Gaunt.

"I didn't hit a damned thing," protested Gaunt. "Blame two heavies with an iron bar."

Cafflin threw back his head and gave a strange, strangled whoop which was meant to be a laugh. Sergeant Cafflin, Royal Tank Regiment, had been blown up by a land-mine in one of those penny-plain, twopence-coloured wars in the Arab Trucial States, where there were always a few British military advisers up front. It had left him without speech or hearing. He'd met Gaunt in military hospital.

But Dan Cafflin could lip-read, he could tune engines by feeling their vibrating life through his fingertips.

Cafflin scribbled again. The car could be ready by lunch-time. He paused, then added another line.

"How much trouble are you in?"

"I don't know yet," admitted Gaunt. "But I'm not making the rules, Dan."

Cafflin looked at him, nodded soberly, then turned his attention to the car.

"How much trouble are you in?"

This time, it was Henry Falconer who asked the question. Gaunt had arrived at the Remembrancer's Department to find one of those "See me" notes propped against his telephone. When he'd gone along the corridor to the senior administrative assistant's office, Hannah North hustled him in, then retired quickly.

"Trouble." Falconer repeated the word. Hunched behind his desk, it was hard to decide from his manner whether he was concerned, angry, or both as he watched Gaunt settle in the chair opposite him. "Your friend Milton called; said he thought I should know about last night. Well?"

"I think somebody feels I'm a nuisance," admitted Gaunt.

"A lot of people probably do," said Falconer grimly. "Some of us have formed a club. Narrow it down."

"Hispan Trading," said Gaunt. "I must have been followed from there—"

"This—ah—" Falconer glanced at some notes—"this John Cass?"

"His people."

"But it wouldn't have looked that way." Falconer nodded, then sighed. "If you treat it as ordinary vandalism, can you claim your own insurance for those headlamps?"

Gaunt nodded.

"Good. We're still in an economy mode." Falconer showed some relief as he turned again to the scatter of papers in front of him. "I've read your report. Now we're sure she's genuine, I'll need to see the Tabor girl again."

"I told her it was likely." Gaunt clasped his hands round one knee and eyed Falconer moodily. "What else do we do about it, Henry?"

"I'm not totally sure." Falconer rubbed his nose as he considered. "The Tabor girl obviously believes Lorna Anderson found a possible pot of gold at the end of this Fraser rainbow." He paused. "But of course, it may not have been Fraser's gold—not all of it, at any rate. His—ah—associates would have been suitably annoyed when he died and they couldn't find it."

"Then along comes Lorna Anderson and she knows something they don't—" Gaunt shaped a lop-sided grin. "I think you've just won a prize."

"Probably something unspeakable and uneatable," said Falconer. He tapped the report sheets. "You say you'll arrange to take the Tabor girl to Fraser's cottage."

"This afternoon, if I can fix it. She's keen; it might be useful." Gaunt counted the rest on his fingertips. "I want to get hold of Detective Sergeant Angus and see if he'll run a check on John Cass. Then there's a part-timer on the Hispan staff called Church; he works from home, handles the property side. He might be worth a look. The other thing—well, how busy are Companies Branch?"

"Underpaid, understaffed, overworked," said Falconer. "Their golf is suffering. What do you want there?"

"To see if Lorna Anderson pestered them—or if they can find anything odd in the Hispan set-up."

"You tell them," said Falconer grimly. "If they even see me they start moaning. I'll handle the police, slightly higher up the ladder than your detective sergeant. This man Church"—he sucked his lips, then his broad, doleful face crinkled in a surprising smile—"Hannah could see him. We—she has been checking on some of those Spanish property offers; she can make prospective-customer noises."

"Why?"

"Because it keeps you out of it," said Falconer. "As of last night, your face is a liability. I need you in one piece for Tenerife—that damned boat, remember?" His face sagged again. "Not that we'll see more than expenses out of it. I've talked with the Remembrancer, he says we're morally bound to hand over the rest to the Tabor girl."

"You don't approve?" asked Gaunt. He chuckled when he didn't get an answer. "Henry, watch it. You could end up robbing orphans."

"Show me an orphan," said Falconer. "I'll think about it."

Henry Falconer began his share of the work by asking Hannah North to look in, and Gaunt left them. Back in his own room, he coaxed a mug of coffee from the typing pool girls, then reached for the telephone directory.

The quickest way to locate the owners of the cottage Peter Fraser had rented was through the lawyer who had handled most of the dead man's business. Another call after that, and he was speaking to a farmer's wife near Bathgate. Her name was Maisie Roberts, her husband had gone out to one of the local markets, and she agreed that Mallard Cottage was their property.

"It's empty at the moment," she said cheerfully. "If you're interested in renting it—"

"No, it's something different," said Gaunt, stopping her. "One of your previous tenants was named Fraser."

"That's right." A note of caution entered her voice. "Why?"

"A relative has arrived from Canada," explained Gaunt. "Call it a sentimental thing. She'd like to see inside the cottage, but it wouldn't take long."

"Another of them?" The woman didn't hide her surprise. "We had a visitor like that a week ago—a Mrs. Anderson. How many more are there?"

"None I know about," soothed Gaunt. "Could we come out this afternoon?"

"No." She was firm. "I'm going out, neither of us will be back until evening. But we could arrange it for then, if it's just a quick look around."

They agreed on nine o'clock.

"But no later," she warned. "If you're not there, we won't wait."

Gaunt thanked her, broke the connection, then dialled Detective Sergeant Angus's office number. Angus was in. He answered his extension with a gloomy lack of enthusiasm that didn't change when he heard who was calling.

"What is it this time?" he asked resignedly. "I've got a warehouse break-in, we're trying to sort out a bus-load of shop-lifters, and there's some damned idiot flashing his way around Princes Street Gardens. Exposure? He's risking frostbite."

"It's back to Lorna Anderson," said Gaunt. "When you talked to her that night, before she collapsed, did she say anything about leaving Edinburgh, taking a plane trip?"

The policeman took a moment or two to organise his thoughts. "I didn't say anything about that in my report—"

"But did she?"

"Yes." There was another, thinking silence. "I made some moan about the weather, she said our snow was kid stuff to what they got in Canada; then she said she'd be in the sun and heat within the week."

"Did she say where?"

"No." Angus was positive. "What's happening?"

"A few things." It seemed fair to give him some kind of warning. "Don't ask why, but keep your paperwork up to date." Gaunt grinned at the policeman's muttered obscenity. "You can thank me later."

He made one more call, the travel agency number Lorna Anderson had written on the Hispan leaflet. The girl at the Universal Travel Agency inquiry desk was friendly and helpful and kept him waiting less than a minute.

They had Lorna Anderson's name on file. She had inquired about both package-tour and scheduled-service flights to Tenerife but hadn't confirmed a booking.

"We told her there wouldn't be any problem," said the girl. "Two people travelling to the Canary Islands at this time of year—"

"Two?" asked Gaunt.

"That's right," said the girl. "Mrs. Anderson said she'd have to wait until someone arrived from Canada."

He thanked her and hung up. Another small but significant thread of the pattern had stopped being a loose end.

Companies Branch came next. They were located on the ground floor of the Exchequer Building, seldom spoke to anyone else if they could avoid it, and lived in a world of indexes and listings. Old wooden cabinets crammed with filed documents fought for space with computer terminals and software. Somewhere along the centuries the Remembrancer had collected Companies Branch, but they never quite admitted it.

The typing pool answered Gaunt's telephone when he wasn't around. He left a message with them in case Lorna Tabor called, to tell her of the Mallard Cottage situation. Then he went down the broad marble stairway to the Companies den.

The help he wanted was in the library area. Annie Blackthorn ruled there. She was tall, angular, grey-haired, and no one could remember when she hadn't been that way. Winter or summer, she always wore dark blue with a single string of pearls. Juniors quaked when she approached, even the Remembrancer was alleged to go in fear of her wrath.

But she knew more about Companies Branch and its workings than anyone else, and she possessed an unerring ability to untangle the most complex company structures and strip what remained to basic fact.

Gaunt approached her cautiously. He always did. She listened, frowning. She always did.

"You want to know about Hispan Trading?" Annie Blackthorn brushed a speck of almost invisible lint from one blue sleeve and pursed her lips. "We looked into that months ago, soon after your man Fraser died."

Gaunt nodded. "Do you remember the details?"

"Certainly." She treated the question with near-surprise. "Hispan is Spanish-owned. They registered a small company here using the same name; there can be taxation benefits."

"Did Fraser have any financial interest?"

"No." She shook her head firmly. "That was what we were asked to establish, Mr. Gaunt. The same applied to a subsidiary of the subsidiary—a property company."

"Hispan Properties." Gaunt sighed. That kind of explanation would have been too simple. "Could you look at both of them again?"

Annie Blackthorn raised an eyebrow but left the question unspoken.

"There's something wrong. Fraser may have been using Hispan, or Hispan may have been using Fraser. Don't ask me to prove it, either way."

"I see." She frowned again, unimpressed. "We can't tell you anything about the parent company. Is the suggestion that your Mr. Fraser was—ah—cooking the subsidiary books?"

"Maybe." Gaunt shrugged. "There's something hidden away somewhere—or that's how things look. It doesn't have to be bags of gold."

"These days, certified cheques are more convenient," said Annie Blackthorn. It was the nearest thing to a joke he'd heard her make. She gave a slight smile. "I'll have another look at what we've got."

"Thank you." Another thought struck him as he turned to leave.

"Has anyone else—anyone outside—been asking about Hispan lately?"

"No." She shook her head. "I would have heard."

He believed her.

There were no messages waiting when he got back to his desk. For the moment, he was in the kind of situation he hated, when other people were setting the pace, leaving him little or nothing to do. He puzzled and doodled, abandoned that to itemise an expense sheet for the Amsterdam trip, finished that, then almost grabbed the telephone when it rang.

The call was from Lorna Tabor.

"How are you?" he asked.

"Fine." She chuckled over the line. "I slept like the legendary log, woke up feeling human again, and right now I'm at the Canadian Consulate. They let me borrow a phone."

"Why the consulate?" he asked.

"Why not?" she countered. "I pay my taxes." Her manner sobered. "Two reasons, Jonny. I wanted to check the arrangements they've made to fly Aunt Lorna's body home. Some of her late husband's relatives want her buried out there, beside him. I thought —well, I should make sure there were no problems."

"They'll appreciate it," he said quietly. "And the other reason?"

"I asked the consulate to give me the name of a good lawyer over here, to look after things for me." She paused. "How about the cottage, Jonny? Can we go there?"

"It has to be tonight." He explained the arrangements.

"That's reasonable. We're asking the favour." She sounded pleased. "How do you react when a lady offers to buy you dinner?"

"I check her credit rating, then say yes." He grinned at the telephone. "I'll pick you up at your hotel, six-thirty. I know a restaurant near where we're going."

"Does your boss still want to see me again?"

"More than ever," he said.

"Tell him today's busy, but I'll be on his doorstep tomorrow morning," she suggested. "Right now, I'm going to see your friend Andy Deathstone. I called him, told him I wanted to ask some more questions about that family tree."

"Why?" asked Gaunt suspiciously. "What do you want to find out now?"

"I don't know," she admitted. "But I've got a strange feeling about it—that it matters." Her voice became suddenly business like. "I've also got an appointment with that lawyer; I'll have to go."

Gaunt said goodbye and hung up.

It was almost noon when he was summoned to Henry Falconer's office. He found the senior administrative assistant standing by his window, framed in the pale winter sunlight, an incipient scowl on his big, broad face.

"I've heard from Hannah," said Falconer brusquely. "She talked to Church, the Hispan Properties salesman—called him at his home number, told him she was interested in apartments in the sun, and he was on her doorstep almost before she could put the phone down." He grunted. "Our Mr. Church turns out to be a retired bank clerk, trying to earn some extra cash. All he knows about the Hispan set-up would leave space on a postage stamp."

"It helps to know," mused Gaunt. "Narrows the options, Henry. Where's Hannah now?"

"Taking the rest of the day off." Falconer wasn't pleased.

"How about your police friend?"

"I spoke to him. He called back, and I've to meet him for lunch; he didn't say anything more." Falconer moved away from the window and became more human. "When are you seeing the Tabor girl?"

"Tonight, to take her out to Mallard Cottage. She said she'd visit you tomorrow."

Falconer frowned. "Keep an eye on her. I'm not in a mood to totally trust anyone."

His telephone rang. Sighing, Falconer crossed to his desk, lifted the receiver, and answered the call. He put his hand over the mouthpiece.

"Annie Blackthorn, for you," he said gloomily. "Why does that damned woman always make me feel I should stand at attention?"

Gaunt took the receiver.

"Hispan Trading and Hispan Properties," said Miss Blackthorn briskly over the line. "I've done what you asked, gone over everything we've got."

"I appreciate it—" began Gaunt.

"I don't think you will," she stopped him. "They file normal trading returns on schedule, they haven't caused us any problems."

"No rough edges?" asked Gaunt.

"None," she said. "Except, if you go by the trading returns, I wouldn't call it a particularly profitable enterprise. At least, not until the property subsidiary started up. It's doing reasonably well."

"What about names?"

"Only one: a Paul Weber, listed as sole proprietor, resident in Tenerife." Annie Blackthorn drew breath, then finished with a final whipcrack. "If Henry Falconer is still with you, tell the big buffoon I'm still short of staff down here."

"I will," promised Gaunt, and hung up.

"Anything?" asked Falconer.

He shook his head. "On paper, they're clean."

"That's when there's usually something wrong," said Falconer. "What else did she say?"

"She sent her regards," said Gaunt.

"I'll try to believe it," said Falconer grimly. He looked at his desk, then at his wrist-watch. "Maybe we'll have better luck with John Cass. You'll be around?"

Gaunt nodded.

"Then this will help you pass the time." Falconer lifted a folder from his desk and handed it over. "Revised security arrangements at royal residences in Scotland. We've been asked to comment." He grinned at Gaunt. "Just give me an outline reaction. There's no rush: any time this afternoon will do."

Gaunt had a sandwich lunch out, then was back at his desk before two. He sat for a while, thinking, getting nowhere, then gave up in disgust and opened the royal residences folder.

Once he got past the long-winded preliminaries, some of the rec-ommendations made interesting enough reading. Holyrood Palace in Edinburgh and Balmoral Castle in Deeside were just two of the places covered. When the Queen crossed the border from England and entered Scotland, some of her own permanent security team followed but the balance became local. In the same way, some of the problems changed.

A sniper with a high-powered rifle and telescopic sights, hidden in a deer forest, was at least as big a danger as someone with a hand-gun, close up, in a London street.

The same applied to the places where she might stay. The army supplied ceremonial guards, the police could chase away inquisitive tourists. But real security meant an invisible web of electronic sensors and monitor devices.

Or it should. There were gaps. Lift a manhole outside one stately home which was a royal favourite, cut a telephone cable, and there wasn't much left.

A lot of money was going to have to be spent. Even then, Gaunt wondered if there could be any real guarantees, if a small, determined team of people couldn't still achieve pretty much what they wanted.

He was still reading when there was a knock on his door. One of the typing pool girls looked in.

"You've a visitor," she said. "He says he hasn't an appointment, but he knows you—"

"And I only want a minute," said a soft, wheedling voice behind her. The smartly dressed figure of John Cass smiled in at him over her shoulder. "Can you spare that?"

Gaunt nodded to the girl, beckoned Cass in, and indicated the spare chair. As the door closed, Cass settled his tall, thin frame and faced him.

"I thought I'd come and see you." Cass looked around. "And where you work too, I suppose." His small mouth shaped a smile. "But mainly to apologise. I more or less threw you out last night."

"I've known worse." Gaunt waited.

"Hispan hasn't many important clients. The man with me when you arrived is one of them, and is short on patience." Cass gestured apologetically with his hands. "You asked about Peter Fraser; I could have told you more, certainly more than I would have told Mrs. Anderson."

"Go ahead," invited Gaunt.

"He may have had his fingers in the till. There were—well, certain shortages when I took over."

Gaunt raised an eyebrow. "Did you tell them in Tenerife?"

"I made that mistake." Cass grimaced. "I didn't realise that he'd been—ah—a close friend as far as they were concerned. I was told that accounting errors can happen."

"Meaning they didn't want to know?"

The man nodded. "That's why I'm cautious when anyone asks about Fraser."

"Let dead thieves lie?" Gaunt kept a tight grip on his reactions.

"Something like that." Cass leaned forward in his chair. "You could also say I like my job."

"How much did he take them for?" asked Gaunt.

"A lot. I can't put a figure on it." Cass shook his head. "Probably as much again as he earned. It isn't too difficult when you're operating so far away from your owners."

"Did he have help?"

Cass sighed and rubbed his beaked nose. "I've no idea. But—well, I couldn't say much to that Canadian woman, could I?"

"A gentleman wouldn't," said Gaunt. He got to his feet. "Thanks for looking in."

"I wanted to." Cass rose then hesitated. "You said there's another relative—"

"We've had an inquiry."

"Well, you know my difficulty. But you can tell anyone who asks that we've nothing that belonged to Fraser still in our office." Cass shaped a rueful half-smile. "And the rest needn't be mentioned— here or when you're in Tenerife, please."

Cass left, closing the door gently behind him, and Gaunt stayed on his feet for a long moment. He swore softly, with something close to admiration.

He'd been conned before, sometimes successfully, by experts. But John Cass had been as convincing as any he'd come across.

It was almost a pity he had to be lying.

Another half-hour passed before Henry Falconer returned from lunch. His breath smelled of gin, and he strode into Gaunt's room with an excited confidence.

"I've got what we wanted on this man Cass," he declared, rubbing his hands. "Out of the shadows, Jonathan, a beginning of reality."

"That's poetic," said Gaunt. He leaned on his elbows and looked up at Falconer. "If you'd been earlier, you could have told him."

"He came here?" Falconer blinked. "Damn his brass neck. Why?"

"Apologetic noises and a story that Hispan wanted to hush up the fact Fraser had been on the fiddle."

Falconer swallowed and sat on the edge of Gaunt's desk. "Did you believe it?"

"No," said Gaunt. "How was lunch?"

"Expensive, but worth it." Falconer drew a deep, satisfied breath and let it out in a new cloud of gin fumes. "My—ah—policeman ended up contacting Interpol. I'll say this much for this Hispan organisation: if they're honest, they've a damned unusual recruiting policy."

"Meaning Cass?"

Falconer nodded. "He's Belgian by nationality, but after that he's almost a carbon copy of what we know about Fraser—on various people's books for suspected fraud, possible fringe involvement in criminal activities, all the rest of it. The only difference is he seems to have moved around Europe a little more."

"Any convictions?" Gaunt felt no particular surprise.

"One, in France. Sentenced to two years for sticking expensive labels on cheap bottles of wine." Falconer allowed himself the luxury of a smile. "He was selling to some of the best hotels in Paris and they didn't spot the difference. He got out about three years ago, turned up in London briefly, then vanished. One story was he'd got to New York. Nobody knew he was in Britain."

"The same man? No chance of a mistake?" asked Gaunt. It was important to be sure.

"None. That's what took a little time." Falconer eyed him blandly. "It seems the Hispan office telephones developed a fault about midmorning. A telephone engineer had to pay them a visit and change the instruments. That way, we had fingerprints."

"You've got a very friendly policeman," said Gaunt, startled.

"All in the interests of justice," murmured Falconer. "Though—ah—I may have told you I was elected membership convenor at my golf club. We've a very long waiting list, but there can be exceptions."

"Bribery and corruption?"

"That's right," agreed Falconer, unperturbed. "He plays quite a good game too." He paused and frowned. "But what about Cass? Why try to sell you that story?"

"It could be his own idea, or he could have been told to spread the confusion." Gaunt winced at another gust of close-up gin fumes. "We're being pointed away."

"From Hispan Trading?" Falconer considered it, then sighed. "I checked on them, pure routine, right at the start—the Tenerife end, I mean. The Spanish authorities hadn't anything against them."

"Maybe you should try again," Gaunt told him.

Falconer nodded.

"And Cass?"

"That's being arranged; he'll be watched only, for now." Falconer heaved a sigh. "Any of these typing pool children know how to make a decent cup of coffee? With Hannah off—"

"Live dangerously," suggested Gaunt. "Try them."

"I will." Falconer got down from the desk. His eyes caught sight of the royal-residences security folder. "Making progress with that?"

Gaunt nodded.

"Any—ah—observations?"

"So far, just one," said Gaunt. "Be glad the national anthem is still 'God Save the Queen.' From the looks of this lot, no one else can."

The rest of the afternoon crawled past without anything happening. At five-thirty, he left the Exchequer Building and caught a crowded bus out to Dan Cafflin's workshop.

The Ford was lying outside the dilapidated hut, headlamps replaced, ready for the road again.

"How much do I owe you?" asked Gaunt.

Cafflin scribbled on his notebook, then offered it.

" 'Bill me for it later, but no charge for the extra,' " read Gaunt, and raised an eyebrow. "What extra?"

Cafflin's oil-grimed face split in a grin, he beckoned, and Gaunt followed him into the workshop. Cafflin pointed to a small metal tube lying on a bench. Capped at one end, fitted with what looked like a release button, it was no bigger than an old-fashioned fountain-pen.

"Well?" asked Gaunt suspiciously.

Cafflin gestured him to one side, then picked up the little metal tube, pointed it almost casually at a thick wooden support beam, and pressed the button.

There was a faint click, then a soft thud as a small steel dart flashed across the workshop and embedded itself deep into the wood. Swearing softly, Gaunt took the tube from Cafflin.

"A damned spring-gun—" He knew how they worked, a tightly compressed-steel spring packing enough energy on release to throw its projectile with killing force, but had never seen one quite so small and neat. "You made it?"

Cafflin nodded and pointed to some fine-gauge tubing lying on the work-bench.

Gaunt scowled. "You know you could land in jail for making that kind of toy?"

Unconcerned, Cafflin wrote in his notebook.

"You said you had trouble," reminded the scrawl.

Gaunt sighed and nodded. "Trouble, yes—but I'm not in a war."

"Be prepared," scribbled Cafflin. "I was a Boy Scout once." He turned away, breaking all communication, and used a small tool shaped like a thin clamp to reload the spring-gun. Finished, he faced Gaunt, slipped the metal tube into his visitor's top jacket pocket, hidden from sight, then raised a hopeful eyebrow.

"All right," surrendered Gaunt.

Cafflin relaxed, smiled, and clapped him on the shoulder.

It was a ten-minute drive from the workshop to the Carcroft Hotel, the evening sky above the city black as velvet and sprinkled with stars. Princes Street was a blaze of lights and the castle floodlights had also been switched on. Gaunt reached the hotel, parked outside, and found Lorna Tabor already waiting for him just inside the lobby.

"Am I late?" He glanced at his watch.

"No, I just don't like hanging around hotel rooms." She wrinkled her nose. "Anyway, I wanted to talk to the girl on the desk."

She seemed totally rested, the tiredness gone from around her dark, lively eyes. Her black hair was brushed high and back, and she wore a purple wool dress with a throat-hugging cowl neck. It was held at the waist by a matching belt with a large silver buckle.

"You look good," said Gaunt, meaning it. He nodded towards the reception desk. "Is there a problem?"

"I don't know." Lorna Tabor pursed her lips a little. "I was out most of the afternoon, but they told me when I got back. A man phoned; he said he was a reporter on the *Scotsman* newspaper and he'd heard a relative of Lorna Anderson had arrived from Canada. He asked if they knew anything about me."

"Did they tell him?"

She nodded wryly. "They said I was here, but didn't give him my name. He hasn't called again—not yet, anyway. What do you think?"

"None of the papers reported her death," said Gaunt slowly. "Did he leave a name?"

She shook her head.

"It might be genuine, it might not." He shrugged, but the possibilities worried him. "If he hasn't called by the time we get back, I can check it."

"And I'm not worried about my room," she said. "Whatever this place was like before, it's security-mad now: they've got staff practically prowling the corridors."

Her sheepskin coat was lying over a chair. She picked it up, Gaunt helped her into it, and they went out to the car.

She was wearing a light, tantalising perfume. It teased at his senses as he drove out of the city, heading west, slotted into a busy, slow-moving traffic stream.

"How was your day?" she asked, curled comfortably in the passenger seat.

"Reasonable." He had to brake as the car ahead slowed. "We're still burrowing, but not getting too far."

"Was Peter Fraser a crook?"

"It looks that way." Gaunt gave her a sideways glance. "Did you know Aunt Lorna was thinking of a trip out to Tenerife—for both of you?"

"No." There was total, puzzled surprise in her voice. "Why?"

Gaunt shrugged. Just about everything ended up with that same question; one single answer might make sense of the whole tangled, uncertain mess.

"What happened to you?" he asked.

"Quite a lot." She lit a cigarette using a match. The tiny flame reflected in her eyes, then went out, leaving her face little more than a silhouette in the dull glow of the instrument lights. "I saw the consul, then went on to my lawyer; you knew about that. The legal side doesn't seem to have too many problems. He says he'll handle everything."

"Then deduct his bill," said Gaunt sardonically. "How was it with Andy Deathstone?"

"That's one amazing little man." She chuckled. "He even bought me lunch. But there we were in his office, and he's dragging out files and papers, showing me chunks of microfilm; I practically know the Frasers backwards. Then he explained about who can inherit what, and I got lost."

"They're called succession rights," he said absently. "It's a jungle." The traffic was thinning and he took the chance to overtake an airline coach and a heavy truck. "The trouble is, most people still don't make wills. They've decided they're going to live forever."

Except they didn't, and the moment one died, relatives could begin squabbling and a lawyer somewhere could order his new car.

Different countries had different laws. In Scotland, succession was an up, down, and sideways affair when there wasn't a will. A husband or wife came first, but didn't get everything. Next in line in terms of legal rights came children; legitimate, illegitimate or adopted, it made no difference. If a child had already died, that same priority could be claimed by his or her children or grandchildren—which had happened.

Then it all jumped back, to brothers, sisters, and parents of the deceased. They were followed in turn by uncles or aunts, then grandparents, grandparents' relatives, and from there into more tenuous blood-line outposts.

Either they all came swarming or you couldn't find any. He glanced sideways at Lorna Tabor and grinned to himself. Or they popped up at the last minute, out of nowhere. But there was something else nagging at his mind.

"That phone call to your hotel," he said. "You're sure this so-called reporter didn't say anything more?"

Lorna shook her head. "The girl who took the call says no."

"Have you contacted any people who knew Peter Fraser?"

She looked at him, puzzled. "Not yet. But—"

"Do me a favour," suggested Gaunt. "Don't rush into it."

He checked his rear-view mirror. He'd done the same thing regularly since they'd left the hotel, in a way that had nothing to do with normal driving.

So far, he hadn't seen those oddly balanced headlamps anywhere behind him—or any other indication that the Ford was being followed.

But he'd been the one who had more or less told John Cass that another blood relation of Fraser's had arrived on the scene. It had happened, there was nothing he could do about it now, and it had him worried.

After last night, he couldn't take chances.

Gaunt shifted slightly in his seat, and the hard, slim metal shape of the spring-gun tube in his top pocket jabbed at his chest. Suddenly, it was strangely reassuring.

Johnstone House was a one-time mansion converted into a restaurant for people who cared about food. Located on a minor road about twelve miles west of Edinburgh, it had a proprietor who made his own rules for commercial success. There was no elaborate menu. Instead, each day, Johnstone House offered a strictly limited choice of courses for an evening meal at a price just on the modest side of high.

They were decided that morning after the best of the day's market supplies had been purchased. Wines were selected from the cellar to match.

Johnstone House considered it knew best. If a guest didn't appreciate perfection, the guest could go somewhere else and needn't hurry back.

It was still early enough for the flood-lit car-park at the end of a tree-lined driveway to be almost empty. Gaunt stopped the Ford in a space near the stone arch of the doorway, came round to help Lorna

Tabor out of the passenger side, and let her stand for a moment, looking around.

"Nice," she said appreciatively, glancing at the old stone walls and high-pitched, turreted roof-lines. "No hamburgers?"

"No hamburgers." Gaunt wouldn't have been surprised if Johnstone House shed a few tiles at the thought.

"Why the hell not?" She gave him a white-toothed grin and took his arm. "And I'm still paying; I've got Expectations, remember?"

They had a drink in a cellar bar which Johnstone House liked to pretend had once been a dungeon. But it had a stone fireplace with a log fire smouldering and smoking up a vast chimney and the old stone-flagged floor, like the rest, had once been part of the original kitchen.

The restaurant was on an upper floor, a long, narrow room with antique furnishings. The table settings were silver, the napkins damask linen, and the oil paintings on the oak-panelled walls included two by Canaletto.

It was still early, only one other table was occupied, and once they were seated the service was smooth and unhurried. Delicately sliced smoked salmon was followed by a consomme, the main course was rare fillet of Beef Wellington, and the wines were a muscadet and a '70's Château Guerry.

They talked generally, casually, while they ate, and settled for coffee after the Beef Wellington; it came accompanied by two tiny silver dishes filled with miniature Drambuie truffles.

"How many more hideaways like this do you know?" asked Lorna Tabor contentedly, settling back.

"A few." Gaunt grinned at her. "For when someone else is paying."

She looked at him for a moment, wisely.

"Andy Deathstone told me you were divorced; I asked him."

He nodded.

"And she remarried?"

"Yes."

It didn't particularly hurt now. Patti's new husband owned an electronics factory, they now had a child, a baby a few months old. Gaunt had been invited to the christening, had taken a gift, and sometimes visited them. The way he and Patti had broken, it was hard to blame anyone; things just happened that way.

"I went through that," said Lorna Tabor. "He was a college lecturer, we thought everything would be roses." She paused. "Well, there's a lot of it about. Now—how far from here to the cottage?"

"About four miles." Gaunt swirled the last of the wine in his glass, watching it thoughtfully. "I'd like to know the real reason for going."

"What do you mean?" Calmly, she opened her handbag, took out her cigarettes, and lit one. "It's the way I said. I just have this feeling—"

"I remember." He considered her moodily. "Nothing more?"

Lorna Tabor hesitated, then reached out and touched his hand.

"Let's put it this way, Jonny," she said quietly. "If and when there is, I'll tell you."

He had to make do with that.

They left a few minutes later. Outside, the car-park was beginning to fill up and Gaunt took a deliberate, outwardly casual glance around as they walked back to the Ford. But there was no dark Peugeot, no sign of anything out of the ordinary.

He remained on guard as they drove away, and Lorna seemed to sense his tension, even if she misunderstood it.

"Angry?" she asked. "There's no need to be."

Gaunt shook his head, then took another glance in the rear-view mirror. The road behind them was empty.

"Just being careful," he told her.

"I forgot." She sighed, came closer, and her hair brushed his shoulder. "Damn all this and damn the Fraser family tree—but don't blame me."

"I'll try," promised Gaunt.

"Thanks." Her lips brushed his cheek. "Then after tonight, to hell with it; that's a promise."

He'd checked the route to Mallard Cottage. It lay at the end of a twisting web of minor roads, through partly wooded farming country. The Ford's headlights lanced along hedgerows, touched on field gates, and every now and again reflected back from small, bright animal eyes watching from cover.

When the cottage appeared, it was small and single-storey, with white stone walls and a grey slate roof. An old Land-Rover was parked at the front door and lights showed inside the building.

They left the Ford beside the Land-Rover and walked towards the door. It was open and the couple waiting there greeted them with reserved smiles, then invited them in. David Roberts was an elderly, amiable bull of a man, in baggy farming tweeds. His wife Maisie, who did most of the talking, was small and birdlike in her manner.

"We don't mind you looking around as long as it doesn't take too long," she said briskly. "This place hasn't been lived in for a couple of months now—and it's a cold night."

Gaunt had felt the chill the moment they'd stepped inside. Lorna Tabor kept her sheepskin coat tightly buttoned as the Roberts began to show them around.

"It's small, of course," said Mrs. Roberts. Standing in the middle of the hallway, she gestured around. "Just one bedroom, the living-room, and a lounge, kitchen, and bathroom. There was a garage—"

"But it fell down," said her husband. "Old age."

His wife brushed the interruption aside and led them into the bedroom. It was plainly furnished, the bed stripped down to the mattress.

"The last people here were a young couple—about your ages," she explained. "But they left before Christmas." Her attention switched to Lorna. "The other Canadian lady who came here—your aunt, was she?"

Lorna nodded.

"She just wanted to see round the place too. I can't say I understand why, but I suppose there's no harm in it."

They moved on. Kitchen and bathroom came next, both equally cold and with a hint of dampness. A glance in each was enough for Lorna, and she was ready to move on.

"How was Peter Fraser as a tenant?" asked Gaunt as the Robertses led them into the lounge, a large room, again sparsely furnished.

The couple exchanged a glance.

"We never had any trouble," said the woman uneasily.

Roberts added, "But he wasn't what you'd call sociable. Kept to himself; didn't seem to have many visitors. Almost refurnished the place on his own, of course. He had plenty of money."

"Any problems after he died?"

"A few," said Roberts. "Ask Maisie; I kept out o' it."

His wife sniffed at the reminder. "The settling-up was bad enough: his things went, we moved our own stuff back in. But first we had people out from his firm, trying to find business papers—turning the place upside-down. Then the cottage was burgled."

"Nearly wrecked," said Roberts gloomily. "Ach, that happens. Somebody dies, a place is lying empty—"

"When did it happen?" Gaunt cut short the man's grumbling.

"Two or three days after the funeral." Roberts scratched his chin. "Not that they got anything we know about."

While they talked, Lorna Tabor had been moving around the room. She had stopped at a small alcove beside the fireplace; her attention seemed fixed on a small, framed engraving.

"Where did this come from?" she asked in a slightly strained voice.

"That thing?" Maisie Roberts joined her. "It was his: one or two small bits and pieces got left behind." Reaching up, she removed the engraving from its wall-hook. "It's strange you should ask. The last lady—your aunt—noticed it too."

Lorna Tabor said nothing but glanced at Gaunt in a way that brought him over.

He saw for himself and was puzzled. The engraving looked more like a photocopy of an original, a Highland lochside scene with a small fishing-boat moored offshore. Mountains formed a background, and there were cottages further along the shore. But the frame was cheap black plastic and the engraving, copy or otherwise, was mounted behind a white board cut-out which filled more than half of the space available.

He looked again. The artist had had a degree of homespun talent, but this was no masterpiece.

"You can have it if you like," volunteered the woman and smiled at Lorna. "Something to take back to Canada with you; you've more right to it than we have."

"And we don't even like the damned thing," said her husband.

"Thank you." Lorna took the frame and moistened her lips. "You've been very kind. I—I think I've seen enough."

Neither Roberts nor his wife seemed displeased. The cottage interior was cold enough to discourage anyone from lingering.

Gaunt thanked them again. Then, as they began to lock up, he went with Lorna to the car. She got aboard clutching her trophy.

"Well?" asked Gaunt as he settled behind the wheel. "What was that about?"

"Not here," she said quietly. "Pull in somewhere down the road."

He set the car moving and they travelled about half a mile through the night darkness, back along the same narrow, winding road. Then their headlights showed a stretch of level verge. Gaunt let the car roll to a halt on the rough grass and switched off.

"I need some light, and a knife," said Lorna in a flat voice.

He flicked on the car's interior light and gave Lorna his small pocket-knife. Placing the frame glass side down on her lap, she used the sharp tip of the knife blade to cut round the thick tape which sealed the rear of the frame, then tugged the entire back free. She paused, then gently eased the engraving out. Turning it over, she inspected it closely, biting her lip.

"I wouldn't call it valuable," said Gaunt absently. "It's more like someone copied from an original."

She didn't answer. Opening her handbag, she produced an envelope, then took out the single folded sheet of photocopy paper inside it. Spreading out the paper, she placed it beside the engraving. Both showed the same scene. But there were heavy, old-fashioned print above and below Lorna Tabor's copy.

Gaunt took them from her, stared, and swallowed hard. The single line of type above Lorna Tabor's photocopy read proudly, "Watermoor Milling Limited, Inverness." Then, beneath the lochside engraving, heading the small-print articles of association, had been penned in copperplate writing, "Matthew Ronald Fraser, thirty fully paid shares of one pound each. May God prosper this venture."

There were signatures below. The date was 1864.

"Where the hell did you get this?" he asked, bewildered.

"Lorna Anderson had the original. She gave me a copy," said the girl beside him almost wearily. "Two Fraser brothers set up business as millers: Angus Fraser was the eldest and put up most of the money, Matthew was junior partner. She said the mill went out of business almost a hundred years ago. That's when Matthew Fraser emigrated to Canada. He was her great-grandfather."

"She asked you to bring your copy over?"

Lorna nodded.

"Did she tell you why?"

"No. But it was the one thing she didn't have with her." She looked at him intently. "I asked your friend Andy Deathstone about Watermoor Milling this afternoon. He said the records show it was a totally private company, that it didn't go bankrupt; it simply ceased trading."

Gaunt looked again at the papers in his hands. He'd seen old private company share documents often enough, worthless commercially except as collectors' pieces. But an old company lying dormant, forgotten—he remembered John Milton's dry advice. According to the Edinburgh stockbroker, a private company could be a perfect way to hide shady money from outside eyes.

Bring an old, legitimate family business back to life and who would pay any attention in the big wide commercial world?

He compared the two copies again, then peered closer, frowning. The copy from Mallard Cottage, everything but the illustration masked off, was still different. The little fishing-boat had a name on her bow; something had been written in very small lettering in the bottom right corner.

"What is it?" asked Lorna, puzzled.

"Wait." He got closer to the car's interior light, squeezing against her, then swore under his breath.

The name on the fishing-boat's bow was *Black Bear*. The message in the corner was short and simple. "To Marta, who will remember the storm. For everything. P.F."

He showed Lorna what he'd found. She moistened her lips.

"Marta—that was the name on the wreath," she said in a low voice. "Jonny, if he wanted her to have that—"

"Why?" agreed Gaunt.

There was a lot to sort out, he had no idea where some of it might lead. But at last it appeared there was something to work on.

"Nothing else up your sleeve?" he asked drily, giving Lorna back both copies.

"Nothing," she said positively.

She was still very close, looking at him steadily. Gently, he brought her nearer and their lips met. Her hand stroked down his face while he held her. Then, at last, she eased away again.

"There's got to be somewhere more comfortable," she said.

He grinned, and started the car.

CHAPTER FOUR

The attack came exactly one mile on. In two stages.

They had just passed a farm lane when the big Peugeot roared out from cover and began pursuing them, ill-matched headlamps glaring, almost blinding, Gaunt used one hand to knock the rear-view mirror to one side before he snatched down from top to second gear and rammed the accelerator to the floor. Engine bellowing, the Ford shot forward.

Lorna was shouting, but he hadn't time to listen. The Peugeot slammed their rear, fell back, then came on again. Gaunt gained third gear, the little car still shuddering, tyres smoking as they fought for grip. A bend appeared ahead. He wrestled the Ford round, losing the Peugeot's lights for a moment. Then the glare appeared behind them again, and Lorna gripped his shoulder.

"Who are they?" She had to shout again to make herself heard. "Jonny—"

"I don't know." He concentrated on the pot-holed road, too narrow for the Peugeot to pass them, a danger in itself at the speed they were travelling. "Just hold on."

Another bend came up. Gaunt caught a glimpse of large, cut logs piled high beside the verge, then steered into the bend.

Like a long, dark snake, a thick, rusty metal chain suddenly quivered up from the road. At steering-wheel height, it spanned between a large tree and a heavy, partly loaded logging trailer left parked on the opposite verge. He had only seconds, knew he could forget about the brakes at that distance. It came down to the piled, heavy logs on one side or a hedge, trees, and God alone knew what on the other.

Gaunt chose the hedge and hauled the steering-wheel hard over. Lurching into a skid, the car swung like a demented pendulum and he heard Lorna cry out as they hit the hedge side-on. Then there was a tree, something like a giant hammer-blow hit the car on Lorna's side, it seemed to leave the ground, and they were rolling, metal tearing, glass shattering.

The Ford came to rest on its passenger side, at an angle, in a ditch. Dazed, thrown forward, left hanging against his seat-belt, Gaunt tried to move. Pain stabbed through his back. He turned to Lorna Tabor and she lay slumped and silent. Then, where there had been darkness, there was light. The Peugeot had arrived and had stopped. He saw blood on Lorna's forehead at the same time as voices began on the road.

"You almost mucked it," said one, hoarse with tension. "You nearly left it too damned late with that chain."

"It worked," said the other indignantly. He paused then added in near awe, "Hell, look at his car—"

"I was doing sixty-five on the clock, he was pulling away from me." The first man's voice steadied. "All right, we'll finish it. You make sure of them, I'll get rid of the chain."

"I reckon they're dead," said the second man hopefully.

"Just do it before something else comes along." From the sound, his companion was already moving. "We burn the car. That was the deal—and the basket nearly crippled me last night. Shift. We don't want an audience."

Hurrying footsteps and the low background murmur of the wind were punctuated by an occasional crackle from the Ford's cooling exhaust. Gaunt managed to release his seat-belt, tried to turn, and something hard dug into his chest. Fumbling, his fingers closed around the little spring-gun tube Danny Cafflin had tucked in his top pocket.

He waited. One set of footsteps came nearer but he was too low down in his seat to see anything until, suddenly, the door beside him was wrenched open and thrown back. The man who appeared there was scrawny and thin-faced, uneasy in his manner. He balanced a plastic container on the car's angled door-sill; then, as the reek of high-octane fuel reached Gaunt's nostrils the man peered in.

Gaunt moved. The man yelped in surprise, his head jerked back, and Gaunt pressed the spring-gun release.

The little tube gave its modest, deadly click and a round hole blossomed high on the man's throat, the sharp steel dart tearing on through soft flesh and tissue, angling upward.

A strange, gobbling sound, like a half-choked sigh, came from the thin figure and he slumped backwards. The container toppled with him, contents slopping out on to the ground.

But there was still the other man, the one freeing the chain. How long would that take, how long until he missed his companion? It took most of the energy Gaunt felt he had left to lever himself out of the wrecked Ford into the spread of light from the Peugeot's headlamps. He fell on hands and knees beside the sprawled figure on the roadside verge.

The man was dead, his blank eyes staring up at the night sky. Beside him the fuel can was still gurgling as it emptied. But close beside it, also dropped by the man, lay an automatic pistol. Each movement a stab of pain, Gaunt grabbed the pistol. It was a nine-millimetre Luger.

He looked around. The Peugeot was thirty yards down the road and empty. In the other direction, the chain had gone. Something moved in the shadows there and he dropped instinctively behind the shelter of the dead man. A bullet sang over his head. Rolling, gripping the Luger two-handed, Gaunt squeezed the trigger twice and the automatic bucked in his grasp as it snapped back a reply.

A cry of pain came from the shadows. There was a moment's pause. A man appeared, one hand clutching his side as he bolted towards the Peugeot. Coldly, deliberately, Gaunt brought the Luger up again.

Another sick wave of pain washed through him. He couldn't hold the weapon steady, he saw his target almost tumble into the Peugeot, heard it start, then it was moving, accelerating. It swept towards him, racing past, and Gaunt steadied enough to squeeze off one more shot at the near-side front tyre.

The nine-millimetre bullet, hitting at close range, tore through rubber and fabric, then his mind registered the rest in a confusion of almost individual pictures. First the tyre collapsed, causing the Peugeot to skid first one way, then the other. Still accelerating, it travelled wildly, totally out of control for perhaps another hundred yards. Its headlamps showed another of those tall stacks of cut logs —and the car rammed the base of the stack.

Cut trees rose and tumbled like matchsticks thrown from a box. They smashed down on the Peugeot and the noise was like a long roll of thunder. When the noise ended, there was no more movement, only the murmur of the wind, and there was only the faint moonlight.

Gaunt got to his feet. Clutching the Luger, he lurched along the road, reached the half-buried car, managed to look into the passenger compartment, then turned away and wanted to vomit.

The man who had shot at him was still behind the wheel. But he didn't look very much like a man anymore. A long, thick log had penetrated the windshield like a great, blunted lance. It had taken the man high on the chest.

Gaunt went back to the Ford, dropped the pistol, and climbed into the wreck again. Lorna Tabor still lay slumped and motionless, but she was breathing. He tried to move her, but couldn't. No strength left, he let his head fall against the steering-wheel.

Something was coming along the road. He was vaguely conscious of its lights, heard the engine, and the vehicle halted. There were hurrying footsteps and voices, and the voices were somehow familiar. The voices came nearer, there was a gasp, then a hand tugged at his shoulder.

He raised his head. Maisie Roberts was staring at him, wide-eyed. Her big farmer husband stood behind her; their old Land-Rover was a few yards away.

"What happened, Mr. Gaunt?" The woman peered past him then gave another sharp intake of breath. "David, the girl—"

"She's trapped," Gaunt managed to croak. "Get a doctor. Police too—"

"We will." The woman's husband eased her aside and saw for himself, and his mouth tightened briefly. Then his large, strong hands gathered Gaunt up and helped him out, half supporting him. "What about that car along the road?"

Gaunt shook his head. Then the world began to spin, and he fainted.

He came round briefly, in an ambulance. They were travelling fast, the ambulance siren was wailing, and an attendant was bending over the stretcher berth on the other side of the vehicle. The man moved and he saw Lorna was there. Her dark hair was matted with blood and her face, which had been cleaned, was deathly white. Her eyes were closed.

Then the darkness came in again.

Later, he was in a hospital bed. This time he felt better and stayed awake for a spell. The world seemed interspersed between doctors and nurses and police in uniform who seemed to increase in rank with every visit. He was vaguely aware that Falconer was there too.

There were questions, quiet, sympathetic, but insistent. He tried to ask about Lorna Tabor, but didn't get a real answer.

He got angry then, and the pain came back. The police uniforms vanished; a woman doctor in a white coat was bending over him with a nurse in the background.

"I know," soothed the woman doctor. "Don't worry. She'll make it, Mr. Gaunt."

Then he felt a prick in his arm and all he wanted to do was sleep.

When he wakened again his body seemed to ache all over, but he still felt better. He was in a private room, there was daylight outside, and the cool, starched staff nurse who came in was friendly. He was in Edinburgh Royal, it was midmorning, and, medically, there wasn't much wrong with him.

"Slight concussion, a lot of bruising and a cracked rib," she said cheerfully, checking his pulse rate finger-and-thumb-style. Finished, she gave him a smile. "We know about your back; it may feel tender for a spell, but there's no damage."

"That helps." His lips felt dry, there was water in the jug beside his bed, but he had to know about Lorna first. "I had a passenger—"

"The Canadian girl." The staff nurse looked away and spent a moment busily straightening his sheets. "I—well, I'm afraid she needed surgery, Mr. Gaunt." Then she paused and gave him a quick, professional smile. "She came through it all right, don't worry about that."

"How is she?" persisted Gaunt. The staff nurse didn't answer and made a pretence of smoothing one of the sheets again. He seized her wrist. "I want to know."

"They're not certain, it's early yet." She tried to release her wrist then gave up. "I know there's a neuro consultant coming in later.

Maybe after he's been—" she paused again, sympathy in her eyes. "Miss Tabor was brought in with head, leg, and apparent pelvic injuries, none of them really serious. But there's some possible damage to the spinal nerves. You—well, you've been through that."

Staring at her, Gaunt let go.

"I'm sorry," she said.

"Can she—will she be able to walk?" He struggled up on his elbows. The world went into an immediate slow spin and he had to sink down again.

"They don't know," said the staff nurse quietly.

She left. Numbed, Gaunt lay staring at the ceiling. Old memories came back, memories of the fear he had felt while he had waited, his back injured and the future uncertain. It had been a long, agonising wait until at last they'd told him he'd been lucky. Afterwards, alone, he'd wept with relief.

He knew Lorna Tabor had courage. She would need it.

A doctor arrived a little later, poked him, prodded him, made a few satisfied grunts, then left without any attempt at conversation. A young orderly brought him something to eat—scrambled eggs on toast and lukewarm tea—and giggled when he asked whether it was breakfast or lunch.

He had eaten and had pushed the tray aside when Henry Falconer walked in. Falconer looked tired. He gave Gaunt a small, tight smile, sat on the edge of the bed in a way that made it creak, and gave the room a cursory glance. His big, heavy face was grim.

"You know about the girl." He made it a statement.

Gaunt nodded.

"The consultant they're bringing in is good—the best," said Falconer. "I've advised her father and he's flying over. You'll be kept here until tomorrow for observation, then discharged unless anything goes wrong." He shrugged. "And the rest is a mess, agreed?"

"Total," said Gaunt.

"However, we're having co-operation from the police and some other people." Falconer considered a spot on the opposite wall and scowled. "We got some garbled rubbish from you last night— enough to get us started. But I want it again, from the beginning."

Gaunt told him. It seemed to take a long time, and he felt

strangely exhausted at the finish. Falconer sat silent for a moment, then asked a few questions. The answers seemed to satisfy him.

"There's a lot to be done. I'll get on with it." He rose as he spoke. "Officially, all that happened last night was that two men were killed when their car went out of control and crashed. No other vehicle was involved. You understand?"

"Yes." Gaunt nodded wearily. "Henry, about Lorna—"

"I told you. The man seeing her is the best." Falconer went to the door, opened it, then glanced back. "You know, you look bloody awful."

"I feel it," admitted Gaunt.

"That's usually a good sign," said Falconer drily. "By the way, your car is a write-off. You'll have to think up some interesting story for your insurance company."

He went out, the door closed, and Gaunt was left alone again.

He slept for a spell, ached much as before when he wakened, but he could think more clearly. The staff nurse returned. She wanted him up into a chair but he insisted on walking around the room first.

"Not bad," said the staff nurse approvingly. "Now do it again."

He did, grinned triumphantly at her, then decided the chair might be a sensible place for a couple of minutes. The staff nurse helped him wash and shave, considered the results, and seemed satisfied. She produced a dressing-gown from a cupboard and Gaunt saw his clothes were hanging beside it.

"I'll take you visiting," said the staff nurse. "Your friend is conscious and asking for you." She frowned and gave a small, warning gesture. "She's sedated, it'll only be a moment, and she hasn't been told anything." She shook her head, anticipating Gaunt's question. "He hasn't seen her yet."

There were a wheelchair outside and an orderly waiting. Wrapped in the dressing-gown, Gaunt found himself propelled along a maze of hospital corridors and they arrived at a women's surgical ward. The ward sister and Gaunt's staff nurse had a brief, murmured conversation, then he was wheeled into one of the side rooms.

"You've a visitor, Miss Tabor," said the ward sister cheerfully. Then she glanced at the orderly and nodded, and they went out.

Lorna Tabor lay very still on the bed, her dark hair almost covered in bandages, a saline drip connected to one arm, her strong, tanned face strangely drained of colour against the white of the pillows. For a moment Gaunt thought she was asleep. Then her eyes opened, she looked at him, and her mouth shaped an attempt at a smile.

"Hi." It wasn't much more than a whisper. "I like the wheels. You're okay?"

"Just dented." Carefully, Gaunt got himself out of the chair, bent over the bed, and kissed her on the cheek. "You?"

"I don't feel much." She gave a puzzled grimace. "I suppose they've got me doped—"

"To the eyeballs," agreed Gaunt softly.

"But we made it." She let her eyes close. "We were pretty lucky." "Yes."

"Why, Jonny?" She looked at him again, pleading. "Was it that damned Fraser thing?"

He nodded.

She sighed and her eyes closed again.

The room door opened, the orderly and the ward sister came in. Ignoring the wheelchair, Gaunt walked past them.

"Jonny." The whisper reached him at the door. "See you."

"Soon," he promised and went out.

He made it back to his own room, the empty wheelchair following close behind. Then he was glad to get back into bed, glad to be left alone for another spell.

Dusk was greying the sky when the same staff nurse as before looked in. She wore an outdoor coat over her uniform.

"I'm going off duty now." She came over, stood beside the bed and automatically smoothed a wrinkle from the sheets. "I thought you'd want to know—about Miss Tabor. They've decided to operate again."

"When?"

"Tomorrow sometime. Then—well, it'll be a few days." She gave him a small, encouraging smile. "The consultant seems to think there's a good chance."

"Thanks for telling me," said Gaunt.

"They say a very good chance." She glanced at her wrist-watch and winced. "I've a bus to catch. Good luck, Mr. Gaunt."

Time dragged. A new nurse brought him an evening meal, another doctor looked in for about ten seconds. He got up, made a brief, exploring expedition along the corridor, and was chased back to bed by an indignant night sister.

Then at 8 P.M. he had a surprise visitor. Hannah North swept in, carrying a plastic shopping bag.

"I'm here because I was sent." She settled in the chair, inspected Gaunt for a moment, then allowed herself a slight chuckle. "I was told you looked pretty awful. I don't see much difference."

"Thanks." Gaunt found himself grinning. "What's been happening?"

"A lot." Hannah took time to loosen the fastenings of her fur jacket. It looked like mink; he hadn't seen it before. "I've to tell you that Henry can't make it here tonight. You're still being discharged tomorrow and a car will collect you at 10 A.M."

"Fine." He propped himself up on one elbow. "I want to hear the rest of it, Hannah. You usually know more than most people."

"Sorry, not this time. He'll tell you tomorrow," she said primly, but a brief twinkle showed in her eyes. Gaunt suddenly realised that when that twinkle showed or when Hannah North smiled she was a particularly attractive woman. She pursed her lips for a moment. "But I can tell you this much, Jonny. You haven't done anyone's blood pressure much good."

"I didn't plan any of this," said Gaunt.

"I know." She said it soberly. "I'm sorry about the girl, Jonny."

He nodded, with a feeling she meant it.

"How about my car?" It was something to say.

"We got your friend Dan Cafflin to haul it in. He asked me to bring you something." Hannah opened the shopping bag, took out a brown paper parcel tied with string, and laid it on the bed. Then she brought out another package. "And maybe this will help pass some time; I always bring gifts to the sick and needy."

"Thanks, Hannah." He felt touched.

"I'll try and get it back in expenses." She got to her feet and fastened the mink jacket. "Sleep well, Jonny."

Once she had gone, Gaunt reached for the packages. The one sent by Dan Cafflin had a faint scent of engine oil in its wrappings. When he got it open, it held a quarter bottle of malt whisky. He grinned then explored Hannah's package. Tied with gift-wrap ribbon, it was a book on the history of jazz. He wondered how she'd known it would interest him.

But he'd have been even happier if she had told him what was going on.

There was rain pattering on the window when he was wakened the next morning. A doctor came in after breakfast, an elderly man who chain-smoked while he prodded and pummelled.

"Right." The doctor lit a fresh cigarette from the stub of its predecessor and sat on the edge of the bed. "You'll do. In an ideal world, I'd prescribe a week or so rest, no physical or mental strain, and similar rubbish. We don't strap up cracked ribs any more; nature's happier that way." He eyed Gaunt with a mild interest. "You've a prescribed supply of pain-killers, for your back?"

Gaunt nodded.

"Army style." The doctor snorted. "I wouldn't prescribe them for a horse. But keep them handy, as before, be ready to feel stiff and sore for a day or two, and count yourself damned lucky." He drew on his cigarette, coughed, then ordered, "Stand up straight, then touch your toes."

Gaunt obeyed and stifled a yelp as his bruised muscles stabbed an indignant protest.

"That's what I mean," said the doctor amiably. He got up to go. "We're running more tests on Miss Tabor, to make sure we've got the complete picture, then surgery this afternoon, tomorrow at the latest. So no visitors; sorry."

The man left. Gaunt stood at the window for a spell, looking out at the rain. Then, with plenty of time in hand, he got his clothes from the cupboard and dressed. They'd been sponged and brushed but there were some small stains of blood, Lorna's blood, on the jacket and he found some tiny fragments of glass still clinging to the material.

He was in a sober mood when he left the hospital at 10 A.M. An Exchequer Office car and driver waited for him outside and they purred their way through the wet streets of the capital, through the normality of Saturday shopping crowds and umbrellas, hooting taxis, and lumbering buses. It was a different world, maybe the real world, but for the moment Gaunt knew it was no longer his.

He was in the Remembrancer's Department a few minutes before ten-thirty. Because it was Saturday there were few staff around, but Hannah North was at her desk outside Falconer's room. She greeted him with a slight smile, but made no comment and told him to go straight in.

Henry Falconer already had a visitor. There were three chairs round a table in the middle of the room, where a pot of coffee was waiting.

"Good." Falconer looked him up and down and seemed satisfied. He turned to the stranger beside him. "Jonathan, this is Detective Superintendent Afton. He's been—ah—taking an interest on our behalf."

"Lambert Afton." The policeman eyed Gaunt quizzically while Falconer steered them over to the table. As they sat down he said, "You've caused some turmoil, Gaunt."

"I didn't look for it," said Gaunt.

Falconer made a general clucking noise which could have been agreement or the opposite, and poured them coffee. It gave Gaunt a moment to study Afton. The detective superintendent was a tall, grey-haired man in his late forties. He had a thin, calm face, deceptively sleepy-looking eyes, and a brand-new golf club tie identical to the one Falconer wore.

"Shall we start?" asked Falconer and took it for granted his guests agreed. "I think the first thing, Jonathan, is bring you up to date. Thursday night—for the moment that stays a simple road accident, as I suggested."

Gaunt glanced at Afton. "How did you square it?"

"Temporarily and with some difficulty," said the policeman. "Particularly when we'd one dead body a hundred yards away from another." He put a hand in his pocket, drew it out, flicked, and the tiny spring-gun tube rolled across the table. "Yours?"

Gaunt didn't answer.

"Concussion is bad for the memory," said Afton with a studied solemnity. He picked up the little tube again. "Well made—about the best I've seen, and I'd better keep it. You think you'll remember most other things?"

"I believe he will," said Falconer stonily.

"That'll do me for now." Afton shrugged. "Humanity hasn't suffered any particular loss. The man in the car was a Frankie Marcus, according to his fingerprints. The other was called Josh Reilly. Two total nasties, straight out of rent-a-thug, both of them ready to kill if the price was right."

"Nothing to tell us who employed them," said Falconer. He sipped his coffee, the cup held neatly between finger and thumb. "But that thing they had across the road was a logging drag-chain. If you'd hit it, neither of you would have lived."

"They didn't do too badly," said Gaunt bitterly. "Henry, why the cover-up job on it?"

"To buy some time; I thought I explained that yesterday," said Falconer patiently, as if addressing a backward pupil. "The Mallard Cottage people who found you agreed to co-operate, so did the hospital authorities. We even got the kind of newspaper stories we wanted and a mention on local radio—"

"The Peugeot went out of control, probably on a patch of black ice," said Superintendent Afton, his sleepy eyes almost closed. "It happens."

Gaunt nodded. He could appreciate it had meant fast and considerable work.

"But suppose someone tries Lorna's hotel?" he asked.

"Someone has," murmured Falconer. He folded his arms. "Your alleged newspaper reporter telephoned twice yesterday—once in the morning, then in the late afternoon. We had the hotel organised. First, Miss Tabor was out. Second time, she had finished her business, had paid her bill, and had left—going down to London first, then flying back to Canada." Slight amusement entered his voice. "We've something even more positive as far as you're concerned. John Cass of Hispan Trading came here yesterday afternoon, wanting to see you again."

Gaunt blinked. "Did he say why?"

"To have another talk with you about Peter Fraser." Falconer's big broad face didn't alter in expression. "The front office staff told him you'd taken the afternoon off, to say goodbye to Miss Tabor at the airport."

Put together, it sounded reasonable—watertight, in fact. Gaunt tried his coffee, hearing the grandfather clock ticking away in its corner, knowing both men were watching him, certain there was more to come.

He took another swallow, then set down the cup.

"What's the rest of it?" he demanded.

Falconer and Afton exchanged a glance. Afton gave a slight nod.

"Lorna Anderson," said Falconer. "She was right, there is more money—a hell of a lot of money. The old Fraser family firm of Watermoor Milling may have stopped trading over a century ago. But right now it has about two hundred thousand pounds in its bank account."

"Peter Fraser," said Superintendent Afton gloomily. "The account hasn't been touched since he died, and God knows where it all came from." He scowled at Falconer. "You tell him. You did the legwork—and put the frighteners on that bank manager."

Henry Falconer cleared his throat before he started, then told it carefully, precisely, as if already framing the written report which would have to go to the Remembrancer, then on from there.

He had taken the Watermoor Milling private company share certificate copies found in Gaunt's car. He'd started with an initially incredulous Miss Blackthorn in Companies Branch, and gone on from there.

The old Watermoor company was still listed in Companies Branch records. The Bank of Central Scotland had been one of the little company's original guarantors and Miss Blackthorn had a friend in their bank's central computer records section.

An hour later, Falconer had been bumping north aboard an uncomfortable, knuckle-cracking feeder airline flight to Inverness, to be met by a car. He'd arrived at one of the Bank of Central Scotland's country branches in time to spoil lunch for the bank manager.

Getting at the truth had taken most of the afternoon, while the manager's dreams of promotion faded and reality took their place.

It had begun almost four years earlier—three years before Peter Fraser's fatal car crash.

Amiable, confident, obviously prosperous, Peter Fraser had arrived at the little country branch. He was, he explained, an investment consultant based in London with business interests throughout Europe. But he also had a large sentimental streak, he wanted to bring some benefits to the mountains and glens of his forefathers. The bank, of course, would share in that aspect.

He was planning to resurrect the old and local Watermoor Milling company, set it up as a modern factory manufacturing electronics components. Though, of course, it was the kind of secret ambition that would take time to achieve.

One small, bemused bank manager had the rest of it explained to him. Fraser owned two thirds of the share capital in the original Watermoor company; the certificate was laid on his desk. Fraser would open a current account with the branch: thirty thousand pounds in cash came out of his brief-case. Until the time was right, of course, the electronics factory would remain a dream. But the bank account would be a starting point and Fraser would use it for various purposes.

One fat new account and rosy prospects, the kind that would impress head office when the day came, was too much. The bank manager and his wife were entertained to dinner by Fraser that night and the Watermoor Milling account was under way.

"You can guess the rest of it," said Falconer. "Large chunks of cash paid in at regular intervals, then occasional major withdrawals. But the account always well in credit, no problems—a banker's dream."

Then, suddenly, the regular visits by Fraser ceased. No more cash came flowing in, none was drawn out. Two cautiously worded letters sent to the London hotel address Fraser had given brought no reply. Leaving only the bank account with that two hundred thousand pounds' credit—and one puzzled but not particularly worried bank manager.

"Bank managers usually like references," said Gaunt.

Superintendent Afton grinned. "Money's a good reference, anywhere. Like to guess how much cash passed through that Watermoor private account?" He sucked his teeth and didn't wait for a reply. "Almost a cool million, Gaunt, going in and out like that bank was a revolving door."

"Cash withdrawals?"

"Not the way you mean," said Falconer gloomily. "Foreign currency most of the time—everything from dollars to Deutschmarks."

"And pesetas?"

Falconer nodded.

"What happens to our bank manager?"

"Initiative brings its own rewards," said Falconer. Scowling, he drained the last of the coffee in the pot into his cup. "He'll end up a director or a lavatory cleaner; he broke enough rules to qualify either way."

But once the thing started, Gaunt accepted, it could have gone on from there so easily. Even if the little bank manager had at any time suspected he was at the end of a money-laundering operation, the smoother path lay in letting it go on rather than bringing a large account to a grinding halt.

"No leads, in or out?" he asked.

"No." Afton leaned his elbows on the table. "That's all we've got —so far. Except that Fraser wasn't big enough to run any racket this size on his own. Come to that, the same applies to John Cass. As of now, we're watching Cass. But—" He left it at that with a shrug.

There was another silence and again Gaunt knew both men were watching him, deciding something—or making sure.

The grandfather clock ticked on. Outside, a telephone rang and was answered. He could hear the muffled tapping of Hannah's typewriter.

"What's left is Hispan Trading," said Henry Falconer at last. "Hispan—and Tenerife." He paused. "The doctor who saw you this morning says you're fit to travel. Are you?"

"Yes," said Gaunt.

If the truth was in Tenerife, he wanted it, and not least because he had his own bitter anger to settle.

"Good." Falconer gave Afton a quick, relieved glance. "You're already booked on Monday's flight, they're expecting you out at Puerto Tellas to dispose of that damned *Black Bear*. You arrive, you act normally. But you find out anything you can, any way you can."

"Within reason," murmured Superintendent Afton. "The way I see it, you'll be walking on eggs. It could get messy if they break." He gave a slight, apologetic grimace. "Remember, we haven't a single thing against them. You'll have back-up if you really need it; we'll fix that with the Spanish authorities. But no direct contact."

Falconer surprised him with a beaming smile.

"But there will be an arrangement," he said brightly. "Hannah will be out there."

"Hannah?" Gaunt stared at him in disbelief, then turned towards the sound of muffled typing. "You mean—"

"She's going out on the same flight, she'll be staying in Puerto Tellas," agreed Falconer. "Nobody knows she works here. She's already on record as being interested in one of their apartments—so she's out on a short holiday and inspection trip. She saw their salesman again last night, told him she'd go out." He saw the rebellious glint in Gaunt's eyes. "Hannah happens to speak fluent Spanish. She'll be your link—nothing more."

"Does she know that?" demanded Gaunt.

"Of course," soothed Falconer. He frowned. "What's more natural? You walk into an hotel bar, talk casually to a good-looking woman; I know plenty of people who'd grab the chance."

"And Hannah," said Gaunt.

"Perhaps." Falconer's frown became a scowl at the thought. "Anyway, that's how you'll do it."

Gaunt nodded reluctantly, knowing he was beaten.

The rain was still coming down when he used the back way out of the Exchequer Buildings. A lane led down to Princes Street and he rode a bus from there to Dan Cafflin's canalside workshop.

Cafflin was getting ready to close for the weekend. But his broad face split in a grin when he saw his visitor, then he seized Gaunt's shoulders in a welcoming bear-hug.

"Go easy," protested Gaunt.

Cafflin stopped the hug and frowned an anxious question.

"I'm classified fragile," said Gaunt. "Where's my car?"

Cafflin beckoned. They went out into the rain and along to a row of lock-ups beside the workshop, Cafflin opened one of the doors, then stood back with a grimace.

The black Ford lay inside, a pitiful wreck of crumpled metal, a flattened wheel propped against the driver's door, the whole interior a shambles. Grunting, Cafflin produced his notebook and wrote quickly. He could arrange a decent funeral at the nearest scrap-yard.

Tight-lipped, Gaunt walked round the car once. He had seen enough.

"You know what happened?" he asked.

Cafflin nodded and scribbled again. How was the girl?

"Not good." Gaunt looked grimly at the one-time sergeant. "But we'd both have been barbecued if it hadn't been for you."

Cafflin imitated a dart stabbing through the air. Gaunt nodded.

For a moment, Cafflin moved his lips in dumb frustration. Then he used the notebook. Was it finished?

"Not yet, Dan." Gaunt shook his head. He saw Cafflin was waiting, still watching his lips. "But maybe soon; I'm going on a trip on Monday. That might do it."

Frowning, Cafflin scraped his unshaven chin and left it grubbier than ever. Then he seemed to make up his mind about something. Signalling Gaunt to wait, he marched back across his rain-soaked yard and into the workshop. He was gone two or three minutes. When he returned, he was carrying a small, khaki-coloured canvas bag. Face impassive, he handed the bag to Gaunt.

Gaunt opened it and started at two dark green plastic-cased grenades—standard British army issue blast grenades.

"Where the hell did you get these?" he asked.

Cafflin grinned and used his pad. Souvenirs.

"And what the hell am I supposed to do?"

Cafflin used the notebook, scowled, tore out the page, and tried again. Use them.

He turned, looked at the car, then at Gaunt, and raised a hopeful eyebrow.

"Maybe," said Gaunt, and Cafflin was satisfied.

It was early afternoon by the time Gaunt got back to his apartment. There was some mail behind the door, but nothing that mattered. He laid out clean clothes, showered, made a pensive examination of some of the bruising he'd acquired, then dressed again. Opening a couple of tins in the kitchen, he ate without feeling particularly hungry.

Soon after he'd finished, the doorbell rang.

The man waiting when he opened the door was a tall, grim-faced stranger carrying a raincoat. But he had high cheekbones, dark, greying hair, and steady eyes which told their own story.

"I'm John Tabor," said the man in a soft Canadian accent. "Lorna's father. Your boss gave me your address. Can we talk?"

"Yes." Gaunt held out his hand. Tabor gave a wry smile, gripped it for a moment, then came in.

"A drink?" asked Gaunt once Tabor was seated.

"Scotch—on its own. Thanks." Tabor let the raincoat drop on the floor. "Don't worry, this won't take long."

"I'm not going anywhere." Gaunt brought over the drinks.

For a moment, Tabor sipped in silence. Then he looked up.

"I got to see her. I've just come from the hospital." He bit his lip. "It wasn't much of a conversation. They'd finished the tests, were getting her ready for theatre. Probably I shouldn't have been allowed to see her, but they said five minutes." He paused again. "Then I talked to the surgeon. He seems to know what he's doing."

"I'd heard that," said Gaunt.

"Lorna wanted me to meet you." Tabor took a swallow from his drink this time, then swirled what was left in the glass. "She reckons you're the reason she's alive."

"You know what happened?" asked Gaunt. "I got the outline from your boss—enough for now."

Tabor finished his drink, picked up his coat, and rose abruptly. "I'm keeping in touch with the hospital. When there's real news, I'll call." He gave the same wry smile again. "That's the least I owe you."

The rest of the afternoon passed, then early evening. Gaunt stayed in, tried to watch television, then read more of Hannah North's jazz book.

It was nine when John Tabor telephoned.

"She came through it," he said simply. "Some kind of pressure on a nerve; it'll be two or three days before they know anything. No visitors until after that."

"I won't be here," Gaunt told him.

"Your boss explained." Tabor's voice was suddenly cold and bitter. "I hope your trip works out, Mr. Gaunt. By God I do."

Tabor hung up.

Five minutes later, the telephone rang again. This time it was Henry Falconer on the line. He was at home, he was curt and impersonal.

"Just keeping you in touch," he said. "Superintendent Afton called me. His people lost John Cass this afternoon; it looks as though he decided to disappear for a spell."

"Sensible," said Gaunt.

"But probably temporary." In the background, a woman's voice spoke loudly, querulously. Falconer sighed. "I'll leave it at that unless anything happens. Good luck with the trip and—ah—"

"I'll watch out for Hannah," promised Gaunt. "Good secretaries are hard to find."

"They are," said Falconer fervently, and his receiver went down.

CHAPTER FIVE

Pilots on the big jets rate the late afternoon approach to the Canary Islands, off the north west coast of Africa, as among the most dramatic in the world.

First a strange cluster of low, dark shapes appears far ahead on the otherwise limitless blue of the Atlantic. The shapes grow, separate, and become cloud-capped islands with Tenerife the largest, the bulky, snow-capped volcanic peak of Mount Teide jutting through her clouds. Teide serves as a marker—and a warning. Jagged and ferocious, a whole family of sister mountains, only slightly smaller, lie waiting beneath those clouds. When the clouds dissipate, they emerge in awesome ranks.

Jonathan Gaunt had a window seat midway down the tourist section in an Iberia scheduled service jet, a Boeing 737. He finished his drink, had the glass snatched by one of the scurrying Spanish stewardesses, and a moment later the "Fasten seat-belts" sign flicked on in three languages. Hannah North was somewhere up front on the aircraft, travelling first-class. Henry Falconer had explained it, claiming that Hannah, as a possible property buyer, had to project the right image.

She did. He'd seen her sweeping aboard the Boeing at London Heathrow, though she hadn't given him any sign of recognition.

But it had been planned that way.

Gaunt looked down from his window as the Boeing came in. They crossed a rocky coastline edged with surf, and he caught a glimpse of some of the tall white hotel and apartment blocks on part of the island's tourist strip. Then the flight path swung inland, over barren hills and volcanic outcrops of dark rock, punctuated here and there by tiny peasant villages and their small green patches of cultivation.

The flying time from London had been just over four hours—and forty-eight hours had now slipped past since his first Saturday meeting with John Tabor.

Gaunt had stayed indoors most of Sunday except for an hour, when he'd forced his bruised muscles to life, jogging his way round the nearest public park. John Tabor had telephoned again, but only to report there was no change in Lorna's condition. Later there had been a couple of calls from Henry Falconer, sorting out details for Tenerife, saying that the police, still unable to locate John Cass, had one possible sighting of him driving south, towards the English Midlands—and that there was a growing chance of proving a link between Cass and the two men who had died.

But Edinburgh, with all that had happened there, was now a long way behind and what now mattered lay ahead. Gaunt eased his stiffened body into a slightly more comfortable position as the final approach began. The passenger beside him, a thin, elderly Irishwoman who had read a book most of the way, surreptitiously made the sign of the cross, then looked determinedly at the seat-back in front of her.

A few minutes later they had touched down at Reina Sofia airport and were disembarking into warm, welcoming sunlight. Tenerife in February was like summer compared with the cold and damp of winter in Britain. The air was dry, flowers fringed the terminal buildings and were backed by screens of cactus plants and palm trees.

They were at the south end of the island. Reina Sofia was still new enough an airport to look half finished, and immigration and customs formalities came down to a couple of men in uniform who lounged at their desks and waved people to keep moving.

He caught another brief glimpse of Hannah North in the shaded cool of the main concourse. A porter was wheeling her bags in a trolley; then he saw a man holding up a piece of cardboard with "Sr. Gaunt" printed in bold capitals.

He went over. The man was in his late twenties, thin, olive-skinned with a mop of black, well-oiled hair. He wore a well-cut lightweight fawn suit with a white, open-necked shirt, had a couple of thin gold chains round his neck and a much thicker one at his left wrist, and he gave a white-toothed grin as Gaunt arrived.

"Señor Gaunt?" The man tossed the cardboard into a waste basket and held out his hand. "I'm Milo Bajadas. I work for Paul Weber; he asked me to meet you." His English was faultless, the handshake was light and casual, then he took Gaunt's battered travel-bag. "I've a car outside."

The car was a white Mercedes with air-conditioning and sheepskin seat-covers. Bajadas tossed Gaunt's bag into the rear, held the front passenger door open for him, then unhurriedly went round to the other side and got behind the wheel.

"Good flight?" he asked casually, starting the Mercedes and steering it through the bustle of loading coaches and departing cars.

"No problems." Gaunt settled back, then coaxed his rusty Spanish to life. *"Muchas gracias . . . I* didn't expect to be met."

"Paul likes to be helpful," answered Bajadas. He used the car's horn to blast other newly arrived passengers from their path. *"Sí* . . . and you're here to sell something he wants to buy." He gave Gaunt a quick, sideways glance and chuckled. "I work as his personal assistant, so I know how things stand. You have the legal side sorted out?"

"A few last formalities, that's all." They were on the main road, and the Mercedes began to accelerate. Gaunt shook his head as Bajadas offered his cigarettes. "I've given them up. How long have you been with Hispan?"

"Two years, Señor Gaunt." Bajadas took a cigarette, then used the dashboard lighter. He left the cigarette dangling from his lips. "First time on the island?"

Gaunt nodded.

"I come from mainland Spain, Barcelona." The man handled the car lightly, fingertip style. "Paul Weber's father came here from Switzerland. The locals"—he shrugged—"mostly, they are still peasants. What you would call thick, not too clever."

"Then they must be glad to have you around," said Gaunt.

Bajadas grinned but didn't answer.

Heading north along the island's west coast road, it was an hour's drive to Puerto Tellas. Flat, level, partly cultivated land, the soil poor, light brown, and stony, rapidly gave way to barren, rocky desolation. The road narrowed, climbed, and wound through stark cliffs of black volcanic rock. Occasionally, when the road swooped nearer the sea again, small banana plantations clung precariously to a slope with rusting irrigation pipes running down from some source above. The few houses near the roadside were glorified shacks, with barefoot children playing outside their doors.

Most of the time, Bajadas was content to drive, hum under his breath, and point out the occasional landmark. After a spell, Gaunt was equally content to nod and watch through half-closed eyes.

Yet it wasn't all lunar desolation. To their left, the sea was often near and sometimes a village huddled in a cove, boats like toys moored to a tiny stone quay. But that was the old island. The new could be the surprise glimpse of a concrete-and-glass hotel development—and the main road stayed busy with traffic, from tour coaches to rasping motorcycles and heavy diesel trucks.

Another headland showed ahead. The Mercedes climbed the ribbon of road and topped a final rise, and Gaunt had his first view of Puerto Tellas and its bay.

He was looking down at a wide cup-shaped depression which had to be the collapsed remains of some prehistoric volcano. The northerly half had almost vertical cliff escarpments of rock rising directly from the sea. The rest, to the south, amounted to a fringe of rocky foreshore, then steep slopes, the foreshore streaked with black sand, the slopes partly wooded by pine trees, one large section the uniform green of a banana plantation.

Puerto Tellas itself seemed split equally between the old and the new. The northern, larger section was tourist territory, built around a modern marina harbour with a large stone breakwater, and included a large multistorey hotel building and its surrounding complex. A small, much older stone quay and a cluster of little houses with red tile roofs, the original village, still held out along the southern edge of the bay. But the rest was a sprawl of villas and swimming pools, tennis courts and apartment developments, most of them clinging absurdly to the slopes.

It was all as if a mad giant with a sword had hacked and sliced the original mountains from top to bottom, had thrown his debris towards the sea below, then had left man to come in and do what he could with what was left.

"Welcome to our little empire," said Bajadas ironically, taking the Mercedes down the twisting approach road at an alarming rate. He shaved the stone wall guarding a bend and a sheer drop, turning the wheel casually. "You came at a good time, Señor Gaunt. This is off-season, with not too many tourists around." He chuckled. "You'll see that when they do come, it isn't easy for them to escape again."

The road continued its downward plunge, then reached shore level at the dusty edge of the old village. Shabby little houses had walls which were cracked and crumbling, a single dilapidated fishing-boat was tied to the quayside, and the rotted remains of another lay beached on the shore.

"How long before this part is wiped out?" asked Gaunt.

Bajadas shrugged. "Soon—another two years, maybe. *Muy triste* . . . but that's progress."

The new took over, a broad concrete shore road lined with modern villas and apartment blocks. More were building.

"That's our latest." Bajadas gestured towards a construction site, a two-storey apartment development where cement-mixers were throbbing. "Paul is getting ready to start another, on one of the upper slopes. It has one hell of a view, if your legs last out."

They reached the new village centre. Bare and a few shops clustered around the high-rise bulk of the Hotel Agosto, which had palm trees and a fountain at its entrance. Hannah North was booked into the Agosto, and there was a separate reservation in Gaunt's name. The car didn't slow.

"Don't worry about it," advised Bajadas easily. "Paul will explain." He swore and braked as a group of tourists ambled out in front of them, the men in shorts and sports shirts, three girls wearing bikinis and dark glasses. One of the girls laughed at them. Bajadas forced a grin but muttered viciously. "Dam' fool. Does she want shipped home in a box?"

Gaunt grinned. His real interest was on the small forest of yacht masts showing ahead, at the marina.

"I'd like to see the *Black Bear*," he told Bajadas. "Do you know where she's lying, Milo?"

Bajadas nodded, but gave a slight frown. "Maybe later, Señor Gaunt," he suggested. "Paul Weber first, okay?"

Gaunt decided not to argue. The car turned at a corner where a small bar had tables outside its door but only a few customers. A *guardia civil* in grey-green uniform and black patent leather hat, thumbs tucked in the leather belt that supported his holstered pistol, nodded a greeting. Bajadas waved in reply.

"Stay friendly with the law." He winked at Gaunt. "A good rule here . . . *comprendes?*"

"*Comprendo,*" agreed Gaunt. "It's a good rule anywhere."

The car kept on, passed more apartments and villas, then turned in at a driveway lined by young pine trees. A red roof showed behind the trees, then they stopped outside a large two-storey villa. It had a sun patio, a blue tiled swimming pool, and a terraced garden. As they got out of the car a large German shepherd dog rose lazily from the shade of a bush and growled.

Gaunt heard a sharp chirping whistle, then quick, light footsteps. A young girl appeared from the villa. Barely in her teens, wearing shorts and an old shirt, she reached the dog, grabbed it unceremoniously by the neck, and it turned and tried to lick her face.

"*Hola,* Milo," she said.

"*Buenas tardes,*" answered Bajadas, a scowl on his thin, handsome face. "One day that dam' animal will kill someone."

"Not unless I tell him." She laughed and gave the German shepherd an affectionate hug. "You don't know about dogs, Milo."

"And things can stay that way," snapped Bajadas.

She laughed again, gave Gaunt an interested glance, then dragged the dog away towards the swimming pool.

"That's Marta—Paul Weber's sister," said Bajadas. "She runs wild most of the time."

Gaunt hid his surprise. "She's young."

"Thirteen." Bajadas shrugged. "God help us when she's older; then she'll really be a handful." He gestured towards the villa. "Let's go in."

Gaunt followed him into a cool, terrazzo-floored lobby which had a tank with tropical fish set into one wall. Bajadas stopped at a door, knocked, then opened it and ushered Gaunt through into a large room, wood-panelled on three sides, the other wall a complete picture window. The man who stood beside the window was in his late thirties, tanned, stockily built and medium height. He had thinning light brown hair, sharp, confident eyes, and wore a plain grey open-necked sports shirt and matching slacks.

"So you found him, Milo." He came towards them and shook

hands with Gaunt. "I'm Paul Weber. All ready to sell me one boat, Señor Gaunt?"

"Nearly. Once I get the local paperwork sorted out," agreed Gaunt. "That won't take long."

"So far, it's taken a year," said Weber. He nodded to Bajadas. "Find yourself a beer, Milo. But don't stray too far."

Bajadas left them, closing the door, and Gaunt looked around the room. It was plainly but expensively furnished, a large, paper-littered desk in the middle, armchairs upholstered in dark green leather positioned round a low marble-topped table. Some silver cups and trophies sat on a sideboard, and an architect's impression of a sweep of apartment developments hung above an elaborately carved stone fireplace.

He faced Weber again, knowing the man had been silently sizing him up.

"Yours?" he asked, indicating the trophies.

"Target-shooting." Weber shrugged. "I don't get much time for it now."

"Then how much time will you have for a boat?" asked Gaunt. Weber's eyes narrowed for a moment, then he chuckled.

"Enough. I'll make sure of that. But there are other reasons, Gaunt. Call me sentimental, but that was Peter Fraser's boat; I sailed in her with him. Then I also reckon she'll be a good investment. We get plenty of tourists arriving here who can handle a boat, so I may rent her out." He paused. "Could you use a drink?"

"A beer, if it's handy." Gaunt nodded gratefully.

The stocky figure went over to the sideboard and opened it, to disclose a built-in drinks refrigerator. He brought out two cans, pulled their ring-tops, poured them expertly into glasses, and handed one to Gaunt when he returned.

"*Salud.*" Weber tested his drink, then nodded towards the armchairs. "We might as well be comfortable. Sit down."

They settled in two of the chairs, facing one another across the marble-topped table. Gaunt took a long, grateful swallow from his glass, the cool beer washing its way down.

"Did you know Fraser well?" he asked.

"Better than that." Weber shrugged. "He worked for me, but I'd call him a friend. Why?"

"He left us a few problems," said Gaunt. "No will, no relatives—at least, that's how it looked for long enough. Then one turned up, we started to cope—and she died."

"I heard a little about it, through John Cass." Weber gave a casual nod. "He told me that a second relative seemed to have turned up."

"A second possible; we're still checking." Gaunt injected a suitable doubt into his voice. "She appeared, she made a claim, and now she is heading back to Canada; it'll all take time."

"It would take even more time here, under Spanish law," murmured Weber. He lounged back, nursing his glass. "I still miss Fraser; his death was a loss to us. Do you know much about the Hispan Trading operation?"

Gaunt shook his head.

"The opportunities are limited. Tenerife exports bananas, some fruit and vegetables, sometimes a little wine. But there's less in the way of manufactured products; new markets are hard to find." Weber grimaced. "We're middlemen with not much going for us at either end. John Cass doesn't have an easy life."

"I tried to contact him before I left," said Gaunt. "I heard he was off on a trip."

"Chasing orders; that's what he's paid to do." Weber sipped his beer again. "But we're into something better now, property development. We sell people a place in the sun—so that we can relax in the shade." He gave an amused grin. "I'd like you to sample what I mean, as my guest."

"How?" Gaunt raised an eyebrow.

"I cancelled your booking at the Agosto," said Weber. "I'd like you to try one of our new apartments; I think you'll enjoy it. For meals you'll be my guest at the Agosto's restaurant. That's arranged."

"All right." Gaunt knew that to refuse could have been awkward. "Thank you."

"If you like the apartment, tell your friends," said Weber. "That's all I ask. One other thing: tomorrow evening, once we have completed the *Black Bear* sales contract, will you stay for dinner here?"

"What if something goes wrong?" asked Gaunt.

"It won't. I know the people you have to see, and the local magistrate is a good friend of mine." Weber set down his glass and rose. "You'll be staying at our El Barco development; I can show you it from here." He led the way over to the window and pulled a cord, and the slats of the blind opened. Sunlight flooded the shaded room and he pointed. "Over there, on the slope overlooking the marina."

What Weber casually called a slope looked more like a young cliff face and the apartment block, beginning to take on a pink hue, was built in stepped style, so that it seemed to cling to the rock.

"I have other plans." Weber lingered at the window. "There are seven main islands in the Canaries, and on Tenerife our nearest neighbour is Gomera—smaller, still hardly developed. I own land on Gomera, and Hispan Properties will build there eventually. My father and my stepmother have a house there already." He chuckled. "You would like to meet my father. He is an old Swiss goat: my mother died when he was sixty, a year later he married again, his bride a woman half his age. A year after that, I had a new sister."

"Marta." Gaunt nodded. "I met her as we arrived—and her dog."

"Where Marta goes, Oro goes. She lives here most of the time; my father has enough money to travel and spends half of the year in Europe, with my stepmother." Weber seemed in a confiding mood. "Marta took it hard when Peter Fraser died. He was like a *tío* to her, a favourite uncle."

"Didn't he leave you a problem when he died?" asked Gaunt.

"There was a stupid story that our British accounts might have been doctored." Weber's mouth tightened slightly. "I had the accounts audited. That was the end of it."

"A boat like the *Black Bear* doesn't come cheap," said Gaunt. "Some people wondered how he got the money."

"Some people wonder too much." Weber stayed surprisingly patient. "When I met him, Fraser had just finished a contract in the Middle East. He could afford what he wanted. Should I have asked to see his bank statement?"

The meeting was over. Paul Weber escorted Gaunt out to the car, where Bajadas was waiting.

"Enjoy the apartment and enjoy your stay," said Weber as they parted. He smiled. "I'll look forward to tomorrow evening. I've never owned a yacht before."

It was a three-minute drive to the apartment block, which had a wooden carving of a fishing-boat above the main door, but no elevator. Milo Bajadas took Gaunt's bag and led the way up the long climb of stairs to the top floor. There were three doors on the landing. He used a key to open the last of them, put down Gaunt's bag and stood back.

"Any problems, just let me know," he said. "We have a sales office at the Agosto; tell them, and they'll contact me."

He swaggered off.

Gaunt took his bag, went into the apartment, and closed the door. It didn't take long to inspect his unexpected quarters. The apartment was small but well furnished, the layout studio-style but with a separate bedroom. A large window led on to a narrow balcony which gave an almost bird's-eye view across the marina and its lines of moored pleasure craft.

One was the *Black Bear*. A year spent lying idle, probably with minimal maintenance, wouldn't have helped her general condition. Yet why was Paul Weber so eager to become her owner? Gaunt sighed, looking down at the gently bobbing masts and hulls. After that year—more than a year—could the *Black Bear* still hold some key to the whole tangled mess that stretched from Tenerife to Edinburgh and back?

The thought prompted another, gloomier. If Weber hadn't been able to get his hands on what he wanted in that time, what chance had anyone else?

The man's veiled determination to have his visitor in the comparative isolation of an apartment block instead of the Hotel Agosto was easy enough to understand. Weber wanted to keep an eye on him, and that wasn't going to make life easier.

Gaunt stayed a moment longer, watching the sunset. It was dramatic, almost savage, deepening every moment as the sun's dying rays caught the rock escarpment to the north, colouring the whole sweep a deep red.

Like blood. He went in, closed the window, and explored the rest of the apartment. A small bathroom had a modern shower unit. The kitchen fitments included a large well-stocked refrigerator and a bottom shelf with enough bottles to double as a built-in bar. A gas water-heater, already lit, hissed in a vented compartment at the rear.

Gaunt unpacked his bag in the bedroom. Under the top layers of clothing lay some camera equipment. The camera was genuine. He picked up a cardboard box beside it, a box sealed with tape and labelled "accessories."

The accessories were Dan Cafflin's two blast grenades. Hefting the box, he looked around for a hiding place, then found one in the bathroom, a small ventilator hatch set in the ceiling and held by two chrome-headed screws. His penknife blade was enough to loosen the screws and there was trunking on the other side, with plenty of space for the box. Another minute and the hatch was screwed back in place.

Gaunt went back to the window. Dusk had come quickly, a neon sign at the Agosto Hotel was a bright green slash of colour, and there were lights showing in many of its windows. Hannah was there somewhere, probably puzzled at why he hadn't booked in. She'd have to stay that way, until he knew the kind of ground rules Paul Weber was operating under.

Half an hour later, showered, wearing a fresh shirt and a pair of lightweight slacks, he left the apartment. It was almost pitch-dark and the bright stars in the sky had an unfamiliar pattern. More neon signs had appeared in Puerto Tellas's little tourist strip and the Hotel Agosto had become a white, floodlit pillar in the night.

Gaunt walked past it, just one more ambling figure among the drifting holiday-makers beginning to appear in the cool of the evening. He kept on, leaving them behind as he reached the edge of the tourist strip, and made his way into the old fishing-village.

The lights, the smells, the total atmosphere was different. Small children eyed him wisely from doorways, but always with a vigilant grandmother within reach. Here and there a TV screen flickered behind a window. He heard a woman singing and a baby crying. A small black cat with a white patch on one paw stalked something unseen along the top of a wall, and a boy in a waiter's white jacket roared past on a motor cycle.

The Bar Tomás had a tin roof. Gaunt chose it because the door lay open and the customers, all locals, included two members of the

Guardia Civil. Police, whatever their nationality, were a good guide when it came to eating out.

He went into the smoky atmosphere. The chatter of gossip died for a moment, he drew a few surprised glances, then the Bar Tomás's patrons decided to ignore this stranger and the voices began again. A few small tables were ranged against one wall, under a gallery of magazine pin-up photographs. Four old men were engrossed in a game of cards at one table; the others were empty.

Gaunt chose a table which allowed him to keep an eye on both the door and the bar and sat down with a feeling of relief, the low separate aches in his chest and back reminding him he'd already had a long day. A stained, handwritten menu lay on the faded oilcloth cover and, as he glanced at it, a man came over from behind the bar.

"Señor?" A small, broad-built, middle-aged man with curly grey hair, he had a considerable paunch which strained against a grubby white shirt tucked tightly into dark blue trousers. "You wish to eat here?" He looked slightly worried. "Our food is *guanche*, for local people."

"I'll take my chance." Gaunt eyed the man's paunch. "You seem to survive on it."

"*Sí.*" The man chuckled and relaxed. "There is paella; everywhere has paella. But maybe you would like *sancocho;* it is a fish stew."

Gaunt nodded. The man waddled off to a kitchen at the rear and appeared after a few moments with a laden tin tray. He placed a brimming bowl of the stew on the table, flanked it with a spoon and fork, then solemnly filled two chipped glasses with pale yellow wine from an old mineral bottle.

"*Salud.*" He raised one glass, moistened his lips with it, and waited until Gaunt had completed the ritual. "Tourists don't come this way too often, señor. We don't expect it—not here."

"Maybe I liked the architecture," said Gaunt. How could he have explained to the man that he felt more relaxed, safer, in the tumble-down bar. "Is this your place?"

Grinning, the man rested his paunch on the edge of the table.

"*Sí.* I am Tomás—Tomás Reales." He thumbed towards a younger, slimmer, muscular version of himself still behind the bar. "That one is my son, Miguel; he helps in the evenings."

Gaunt nodded. Miguel was watching them with a degree of suspicion. He had chestnut-coloured hair and a gold ear-ring and was dressed in a black singlet and dark trousers.

"What does Miguel do the rest of the time?" he asked politely.

"Sometimes he is in jail." The bar owner's voice held little humour. "Mostly he works at the marina, or finds work on the building sites." He poured more wine into the chipped glasses. "Are you a tourist, señor?"

"No." Gaunt shook his head. "I'm here on business. My name is Gaunt."

Curiosity partly satisfied, the man still seemed in no hurry to leave. He pointed towards the bar. "The Guardia sergeant saw you in Señor Weber's car. Is Senor Weber a friend?"

"Today was the first time I'd met him," said Gaunt. "Why?"

"We wondered." The bar owner glanced round, pursed his lips, and whistled a few harsh tuneless notes. His son shrugged, seemed to lose interest in them, turned away, and the bar owner explained. "We are from Gomera." He saw it wasn't enough. "At home, on the island, we speak in words, or we whistle, señor. A man can talk by whistling, from one hill to the next—"

"Or across a bar and no one else understands?" Gaunt rubbed a hand across his chin. "What did you tell him?"

"That you were not a friend of Señor Weber." Tomás said it unemotionally. "Miguel has had—*sí,* some difficulty there. So have other people."

"Weber told me his father lives on Gomera," Gaunt said. "He said the family own some land there."

"Not some, a lot," corrected Tomás. He scowled at the notion, then mellowed. "Have you met Marta, the little one?"

"And her dog," said Gaunt and took a spoonful of the rich, dark stew. The fish was sea bass, the rest a thick, spiced mixture of chopped vegetables, the sauce hard to identify but totally appetising. He glanced up at Tomás. "I like it."

"*Gracias.*" The man topped Gaunt's glass again. "So—how long will you stay in Puerto Tellas?"

"A few days," said Gaunt. "It depends on Paul Weber."

The bar owner looked pensive for a moment and scratched at his paunch.

"Maybe I should give you some advice, señor," he said seriously.

"Paul Weber is not patient with people who are difficult. Whatever your business, go carefully." He stepped back and twisted a quick smile. "And next time, when you come, bring a friend. Then you can both talk about our architecture, eh?"

He went back behind the bar. As Gaunt had expected, one of the Guardia officers beckoned and the two men talked quietly for a moment. At the finish, the policeman gave a satisfied nod and helped himself to another drink from a bottle on the bar.

He was left alone after that. Finishing the fish stew, he sipped his way through a final glass of wine then put some money on the table and left. The old men playing cards didn't look up; no one else seemed to pay any particular attention.

A light wind, cool from the Atlantic, had sprung up while he'd been in the bar. It murmured through the narrow streets, banged a loose window shutter somewhere, and brought a salt tang of the sea to challenge the hot smell of the land. Back in the tourist strip, among the neon signs again, more people had appeared at the pavement bars and cafés. Taxis murmured by, disco music rasped into the night.

And he was being followed. At first, it was only a suspicion, a brief glimpse of a figure trailing a stone's-throw distance behind him, a figure who happened to be there a couple of times as a reflection in a shop-window.

He crossed the street and deliberately strolled back the way he'd come for a short distance. The same figure turned on the opposite pavement and kept parallel with him. He was medium height, thick set, and his hands were stuffed in the pockets of a loose brown zip-fronted jacket.

Gaunt loitered outside one of the bars for a moment, then turned on his heel and began walking again. A little way past the Hotel Agosto he stopped and stooped, pretending to tie a shoe-lace. The same man came to a sudden, awkward halt, caught under the glare of Agosto's entrance lights.

Gaunt smiled to himself and walked on, towards the marina.

It had no fence and no gate, just a dusty parking area and a few workshop buildings. The main concrete pier was lit along most of its length and there were other lights all along the curve of the outer breakwater. Floating pontoons extended out from both sides of the pier in a herring-bone pattern, each with a quota of boats creaking at their mooring lines as the black water nuzzled their hulls. Most had been stripped of their deck gear, others lay under protective nylon covers with bare masts protruding as if in protest.

Gaunt walked a short distance along the pier, reached the first pontoon, then glanced round. The lighting around the marina left a multitude of shadows and the man with the brown wind-cheater jacket could have been in any of them. But perhaps he had decided to wait at the marina entrance until his quarry returned. Either way, it hardly mattered. Paul Weber would not be surprised to hear where his visitor had gone.

The first pontoon held a line of small power boats. He moved on to the next, where a big German-registered catamaran was the only one of a row of yachts to show lights. Going past, Gaunt caught a glimpse of a blond woman, totally naked, padding around the cabin.

He checked another two pontoons without success, but a white boat lying isolated and moored bow-on at the next looked a possibility. He went nearer, saw the name painted on her bow, and stopped. His search was over.

The *Black Bear* was roughly as he'd pictured from the few details in the Remembrancer's file. A sleek thirty-foot Bermuda-rig sloop, she had a midships cabin under a smooth fibreglass blister. There was a large cockpit at her stern and a small, upturned dinghy was lashed to the deck for'ard. But even at night, looking at her shadowed lines, he could see that a year lying idle had taken its toll. The white hull was dirty and stained, her deckworks needed painting, her basic rigging hung slack and frayed.

A lot of work would be needed before she was anyone's pride again.

A catwalk led from the pontoon to her deck. Gaunt stepped onto the slatted treads, crossed over, reached the deck, then froze as a rustle of movement reached his ears. The sound had come from the cockpit.

He waited. A fish splashed somewhere in the darkness, then he heard the same rustle followed by a low animal growl.

"Marta?" He called the name softly. "Come on out."

A head appeared at first, looking at him over the cockpit combing. A moment later there were two heads, the other the German shepherd dog, teeth bared, another low growl coming from its throat.

"*Hola,*" he said mildly. "Remember me?"

Marta Weber nodded and climbed out of the cockpit, the dog following her, staying close to her heels, still growling. The girl stopped, spoke in a murmur, scratched the massive head lightly behind one ear, and the dog sat on its haunches, bright eyes still fixed unwaveringly on Gaunt.

"Thanks." Gaunt smiled at the youngster. Wearing jeans and a sleeveless sweater, her long dark hair tied back by a ribbon, she was still very much a child. "Don't be afraid of me."

"I'm not." She scratched the dog's head again.

"Do you know who I am?" he asked.

She nodded. "You're here to sell Peter's boat."

"My friends call me Jonny." Gaunt sat on the overturned dinghy and gave her a moment to get used to him. "What were you doing?"

"*Nada* . . . nothing special." She gave an embarrassed shrug. "I come here sometimes. I like it."

"Good memories?" suggested Gaunt. "That wreath you sent, Marta—the wreath for Peter Fraser's grave. Did Paul know about it?"

She shook her head. "I used my own money. It—did it get there safely?"

"Yes." He watched the girl come closer, Oro inching beside her. "I've heard you liked him a lot."

"Peter?" She gave a slight, wistful smile. "Yes. Did you ever meet him?"

"No. But I knew about him." Gaunt nodded towards the cockpit. "Did you go sailing together?"

"Any time he was here. Paul didn't like it—but Peter just laughed." Her face brightened at the memory. "He said every captain has to have a crew."

"That's true." Gaunt considered the neglected rigging above them. "But didn't he need more help to sail a yacht this size?"

"Peter could handle her." The youngster's voice held a confidence that couldn't be challenged. "Even when we lost the mast in a storm, it didn't worry him."

"When did that happen?" he asked casually.

"Two summers ago." She grinned at him. "Paul thought we'd drowned. *Sí* . . . he almost looked disappointed when we got back. We were missing for eight hours, they had a search plane looking for us."

Gaunt thought of a man and a child facing the angry Atlantic in a boat the size of the *Black Bear* and decided Peter Fraser had to have been a reasonably competent sailor.

"How bad was the damage?" he asked. "You said the mast; what else?"

"A lot." Marta grimaced. "Things were broken, things were swept away. Peter tied me to the rail in the cockpit; I was crying some of the time." She gestured her disgust. "I was younger then, Jonny. Only eleven."

"Much younger," agreed Gaunt solemnly.

He stopped as Oro gave a sudden growl. The dog rose, ears erect, staring at the darkness. Then it began to bark, until Marta grabbed it by the nose. Frowning, the girl peered into the darkness. Gaunt did the same. But whatever was there, whatever the dog had seen or sensed, nothing moved. He glanced at the puzzled child beside him. Even being Weber's stepsister might not guarantee her safety.

"It's late," he said quietly. "Maybe you should go home, Marta."

"Now?" She was disappointed.

"Now," said Gaunt firmly. "But we can talk again, another time."

Marta sighed. Then she went past him and along the catwalk. Glancing back, she gave one of her quick, chirping whistles and Oro bounded to join her. Dog and girl went along the pier and vanished into the night.

He didn't worry about her out there, not with that great, padding animal for company.

But now it was his turn. He went out onto the pontoon and from there to the pier. He heard a soft chuckle, then a stocky figure stepped from behind a small brick store-shed.

"My father sends his regards, señor." The figure halted, grinning. The last time Gaunt had seen him, he had been serving behind the counter at the Bar Tomás.

"You're Miguel, right?"

The young man nodded and came nearer, the gold ear-ring glinting in the darkness.

"What the hell are you doing here?" demanded Gaunt.

"Being a dutiful son." Miguel Reales said it drily. "When you left us, my father saw someone followed you. He decided I should follow him . . . so I did."

"Then what happened?" asked Gaunt suspiciously.

Miguel beckoned, and Gaunt followed him behind the hut. The man with the brown jacket lay as if sleeping, his head pillowed on a large coil of rope.

"He will have a sore head, that's all," said Miguel apologetically. "I made a mistake, I got too close—so I had to hit him before he could do anything." He paused then asked contritely, "Does this embarrass you, Señor Gaunt?"

"No." Gaunt knelt beside the unconscious man. "What did you use—a sledge-hammer?"

The bar owner's son showed his teeth. For a moment a small, leather-bound cosh appeared in one hand, then vanished back into a trouser pocket.

"Do you know him?" asked Gaunt.

"He works for Weber." Miguel squatted down. Quickly and expertly he removed his victim's wrist-watch, then a leather wallet from an inside pocket. He winked. "This way, when he comes round —*es muy triste*, but every now and again someone gets mugged and robbed in Puerto Tellas. Usually a *turista*, of course, but anyone can make a mistake."

"Anyone." Gaunt got to his feet. "Thank your father for his—his thoughtfulness." He pursed his lips. "He said you had run into trouble with Weber. Like to tell me about it?"

Miguel looked embarrassed for a moment, then shrugged. "Sometimes, when money is difficult, I am a thief," he admitted. "Señor Weber is a man with several interests and some wealth."

"So you tried to rob him?"

"*Sí.*" Miguel scowled at the concrete at his feet. "He has a banana plantation, just outside the village. I heard he kept money in the plantation office, and his workers are paid on Fridays—"

"So Thursday would be a good night to find out?"

The man at their feet gave a first, faint groan. Miguel ignored him and nodded.

"The plantation is fenced and has barbed wire; that was no problem. But when I got to the office there were guards—guards, on a banana plantation! They caught me, they had guns, and Weber was there too." He turned and hauled up his black singlet, showing his back to Gaunt. "Can you see, Señor Gaunt?"

Gaunt stared at the criss-cross of healed scars across the tanned flesh.

"They did that?"

Miguel nodded. "Beat me, whipped me, then threw me out. I was to tell my friends so they would know to stay away."

"*Gracias.*" Gaunt drew a deep breath. "Were you inside the office?" The only reply was a headshake, and he tried again. "This plantation—where is it?"

"From here?" Miguel pointed along the shore, to their right. "Ten minutes' walk out of the village, Señor Gaunt. But I crawled back that night, and it took an hour."

The man at their feet groaned again and started to stir.

"I owe you, Miguel," said Gaunt quietly. "Tell your father the same."

They set off along the pier and parted before they reached the lights of the village.

CHAPTER SIX

Puerto Tellas's tourist strip was still blazing with lights and noisy, but Jonathan Gaunt had had enough for one night. He went back to his top-floor apartment in the El Barco building, locked the door, and checked the ventilator hatch in the bathroom. The hatch, with its hidden package, hadn't been disturbed.

The rest of the apartment appeared to be just the way he'd left it. Yet appearance wasn't enough—and he knew where to look to make sure.

He'd left a few traps for any intruder. They were simple enough, they relied on the rule that a careful, searching visitor usually tried to be tidy—and things could be left in better order than before.

The traps had worked, the room had been searched.

A couple of typewritten sheets of paper in his briefcase, left protruding a little from the rest of the contents of a file, were now back in line with the rest. An envelope with the flap only half tucked in was neatly closed. He'd left clean shirts in a drawer, the top shirt slightly rumpled. Now it was smooth.

Even his shaving kit had been checked.

But, apart from the package in the ventilator, there had been nothing to hide.

Satisfied, Gaunt made some coffee in the little kitchen, then filled a mug and took it out on the balcony and looked at the lights below.

Being in the El Barco was a problem. That one entrance at street level, the only apparent way in and out, made it like a mousetrap, but even the best mousetraps had to have a weak point, and maybe he had already seen the answer.

Going in, Gaunt went through to the gas water-heater's compartment at the rear. It had a small, hinged window. Paint flaked from the hinges when he opened it, showing it had never been used. He looked out across a narrow gap at the rock slope behind the El Barco.

The lower levels of the apartment block had been built against the slope. But the top floor was different. Murmuring a thanks to whoever had decided a window would look good there, Gaunt straddled the sill, jumped over onto the slope, and scrambled up from there.

At the top, a small lizard scuttled clear as he crouched down. Where he was, the slope levelled off briefly. There were some trees, then the ground rose again.

The whole vast curve of the bay lay in front of him and, far out, a few bobbing pin-points of light showed where some fishing-boats were working. Another small, isolated cluster of lights caught his eyes. They were to the south, inland, somewhere beyond the village but near the shore. He hadn't noticed them before, they hadn't been visible from either the marina or his balcony.

Paul Weber's plantation lay over there. Someone was working late.

He pursed his lips, remembering what Miguel claimed had happened when the young thief went exploring. What kind of a banana plantation used night guards and handed out that kind of treatment to intruders?

Gaunt stayed at the top of the slope for another few moments, then made the difficult downward scramble through the darkness and climbed back in through the little window.

Now, at least, he had his own back door.

Some of the tension drained from his body, to be replaced by tiredness and familiar pain. Yet Gaunt felt he had made a reasonable start.

He took two of the pain-killer tablets, washed them down with the last of the coffee, and headed for bed.

It was 8 A.M. when he woke. Showered and shaved, dressed again in a shirt and slacks, he went out on the apartment balcony.

For a few minutes, Gaunt forgot why he was in Puerto Tellas and how much still had to be done. The sky was a cloudless blue, the air was fresh and already warm, and the sun had just begun to appear above the high curtain of the rock escarpment.

But it was the sea which held him. A gentle swell was coming in, creaming against the shore, and far out in the bay a school of dolphins were heading south. Fifteen to twenty in number, leaping and sporting, they travelled fast on the same steady course, linked by instinct, totally sure of their purpose.

Gaunt watched until they had gone from sight, then heard voices below him. A couple were having breakfast on one of the lower balconies, ordinary, pleasant-looking people. He switched his attention to the street. It was still quiet, but he felt sure that someone was down there somewhere, watching him.

He checked carefully and spotted a man lounging in a patch of shade. Suddenly, the man moved as a girl came hurrying along the street. They met, got into a parked car, and drove off. Gaunt grinned and gave up.

He waited until 9 A.M., then collected his brief-case, left the apartment building, and walked across to the Hotel Agosto. Breakfast was being served in a terrace beside the pool and when he gave his name to a waiter he was shown to a table. Gaunt ordered coffee, toast, and orange juice, ate slowly, and watched a first few swimmers plunge into the pool. He got up and went into the hotel.

No one seemed to follow him. He made a leisurely tour through the lobby and lounges, looked at the display in the hotel shop, and noted the Hispan Properties office in a corner, still closed; then he found a house phone, asked the operator for Hannah North's room, and waited.

Hannah answered at last, yawning. But she came totally, indignantly awake when she heard his voice.

"Where the hell have you been?" she demanded. "You could have been dead in a ditch for all I knew!"

"Weber changed things for me." Gaunt sketched what had happened, including the marina encounter. "Could I have done it any other way?"

Hannah paused. "Probably not." Gaunt heard the click of a cigarette lighter. "All right, you had problems. I've made contact with the friendlies here: they're not happy, but they'll co-operate. What help do you need?"

"Right now?" He'd puzzled over that himself. "I need to win

some time, Hannah. By tonight, I'm supposed to sign over that boat to Weber—"

"Unless we can stall it. Why not?"

"Fine," said Gaunt acidly. "But how? He could go for my throat."

"We could make it someone else's—keep yours for later." She paused again, thinking. "Look, I know the permissions and clearances you've to get. Which comes last?"

Gaunt scowled at the house phone. "The local magistrate—his official seal. That'll be no problem. He's friendly with Weber."

"What's his name?"

He had to check the prepared list in his pocket. "José Martínez, in Avenida Atlántico. But—"

"Stop saying 'but,' Jonny," said Hannah North patiently. "I'll work out something. Just be good and do what the list says. If you're back here around 2 P.M you'll probably find me around the pool."

"How about floating in it, face-down?" suggested Gaunt.

"I've better plans," she said tolerantly, and hung up.

He left through the hotel lobby. It had a marble fish-pond and a central fountain, and a small boy, escaped from his parents, was leaning over the edge and tormenting the small fish darting frantically in the water.

"Having fun?" asked Gaunt.

"Yes." The boy grinned at him.

"As much as look at those fish again and I'll kick your tail in," said Gaunt softly. "Move, you little monster."

Open-mouthed, the child backed away, stumbled on the edge of the stonework, almost fell into the water, then turned and ran. Feeling better, Gaunt went on his way.

He had four calls to make and they were all within walking distance. First on the list was the government tax official for the district. The man had a cool, air-conditioned office above one of Puerto Tellas's two banks. The man wore a dark jacket and tie to emphasise his official status, sat behind a desk almost the size of a football field, and insisted on reading his way through every line of the already agreed documents Gaunt placed in front of him.

At last, reluctantly, he rang for an assistant, signed the papers, and had them witnessed. The *Black Bear* and the estate of the late Peter Fraser were officially clear of all Spanish taxation claims.

The marina manager came next. A balding, middle-aged expatriate Englishman, Gaunt found him stripping down a boat engine in a shed behind the marina office. Abandoning the engine, wiping his hands on a rag, he led the way through to an untidy shambles of a room, offered Gaunt a seat and a can of beer, opened one for himself, then burrowed among the litter of yachting literature, bills, and correspondence piled on an old kitchen table.

"Got it." Triumphantly, he dragged out a badly typed invoice on the marina company's headed paper. "That's our final account of charges, including berthage until the end of the month. You sign this, I'll sign your release. Fair?"

Gaunt glanced at the charges, decided the marina were making a fast final killing, but didn't argue. Once he'd signed, the marina manager cheerfully did the same to the release forms.

"That damned *Black Bear* hasn't been any asset to the scenery, rotting out there," he confided. "Your people are selling to Paul Weber, right?"

Gaunt nodded.

"He can afford her." The man grinned. "I tried to steer him onto a couple of better buys—bargain offers, Mr. Gaunt. But he wanted that boat, nothing else."

"Did he say why?" asked Gaunt.

"No—and all he knows about sailing wouldn't get him round a bath-tub. But with Weber, you don't ask." The marina manager took another mouthful of beer. "Still, when he's owner that should scare off the local criminal element. You knew we had trouble that way?"

Gaunt showed his surprise. "With the *Black Bear?*"

The man nodded. "Twice in the month after Fraser died, an overnight job each time. The vultures broke into her cabin, practically ripped every fitment apart." He shrugged. "Maybe it should have been an insurance situation, but nobody knew what had been stolen—if anything. So we did a patch-up job, minimum charge, and left it at that. The charge is on your bill, friend."

They talked a little longer but the man couldn't help further, wasn't particularly interested. It was the first Gaunt had heard of the yacht being raided: Weber hadn't mentioned it, there hadn't even been a hint in Henry Falconer's file.

Another short walk and he was at his third destination. Spanish law demanded that legal documents binding within their territory had to be drawn up by a Spanish attorney. All the arrangements had been made from Edinburgh, the contract for sale had been prepared by the Puerto Tellas lawyer, complete with duplicates and English translations. But first Gaunt was kept sitting in a waiting-room for half an hour, then the small, gloomy, chain-smoking *abogado* concerned took as long again mumbling and muttering his way through the collection. Eventually, reluctantly, he finished, scribbled his initials on each page, signed the last with a flourish, then didn't waste energy in rising or saying goodbye when Gaunt left.

It was close to midday, the streets were hot and dusty, and the temperature had to be in the high eighties. Gaunt felt his shirt sticking to his back with sweat as he found the Avenida Atlántico and reached the last address on his list. Señor José Martínez, magistrate for Puerto Tellas and its surrounding district, lived in a large villa. The perimeter walls were a mass of purple bougainvillaea, a large brass plate by the iron gates proclaimed his importance, and a private pool and tennis-court took up a large slice of the garden area.

The young male secretary who came to the door looked flustered when he saw the visitor.

"*Buenos días.*" He gave Gaunt an awkward smile. "Señor Gaunt, we expected you, of course. But—"

"If it helps, I can come back later," suggested Gaunt.

"It will have to be tomorrow." The young man gestured his embarrassment and came out on to the porch. "Señor Martínez has been summoned to the Governor's office in Santa Cruz, on official business. It was unexpected, a matter of urgency—"

"When did he hear?" asked Gaunt unemotionally.

"Less than an hour ago, by telephone. He had to leave by car, immediately. There was no warning."

"Don't worry," soothed Gaunt, straight-faced. Hannah North's ability to make things happen left him stunned. "Tell Señor Martínez I'll call again tomorrow." But he knew he had to be sure. "I have these papers to be notarised. Perhaps another magistrate—?"

"No, Señor Gaunt." The answer left no room for doubt. "Señor

Martínez knows the situation, has been involved. Anyone else would require time to study each document, perhaps obtain additional confirmation."

It was all he needed. He left the villa and walked back along the tourist strip to the Hotel Agosto.

The Hispan Properties sales office in the hotel lobby was open for business but empty of customers. The plump Spanish girl behind the desk smiled when he asked for Milo Bajadas and murmured into a telephone; Bejadas emerged from a private office at the rear.

"*Hola.*" His thin, tanned face split in a white-toothed grin as he came over. "Everything okay now, Señor Gaunt? Work over, and you can relax until tonight, eh?"

"No." Gaunt shook his head sadly. "There's a hitch."

The grin vanished. "Impossible. You told Paul—"

"His tame magistrate has been summoned to Santa Cruz," said Gaunt brutally. "When or if he gets back tomorrow, I can have the papers stamped. Not before."

Bajadas chewed his lower lip and looked worried. "Paul won't be happy."

"He's your magistrate, not mine," shrugged Gaunt. "Don't blame me."

"Okay." Bajadas sighed and ran a hand over his long black hair. "Paul is over at the plantation. I'll tell him when he gets back."

"I could take a taxi over," volunteered Gaunt.

"Better not." Bajadas shook his head then forced a smile. "Out there is *privado*—no visitors, and an awkward gateman. Anyway, Señor Gaunt, I forgot. Paul planned to go on from there, to view some building plots that could be for sale."

"All right." Gaunt didn't have to feign his disappointment. "Then you can help me with something else. I'm no expert on boats, but I still haven't been aboard the *Black Bear*. I took a look at her last night, from the quayside. But I want to be able to say I looked her over when I get back home."

"You mean now?" Bajadas glanced at his gold wrist-watch first, then nodded. "I have a prospect, a woman, to take round some of the apartments. But I can spare a little time. Do you want to see below deck?"

"Yes."

"We can pick up a key." He turned, spoke briefly to the girl at the enquiry desk, then touched Gaunt's arm. "Let's go."

Milo Bajadas seemed to know most people on the short walk from the hotel to the marina basin. Every few yards was punctuated by a wave, a smile, or an exchange of greetings.

"You're popular," said Gaunt drily.

"Part of my job." Bajadas took it as a compliment. "Paul Weber is the kind who prefers to stay in the background. He likes to have—well—"

"Front men?" suggested Gaunt. "Was that how he used Peter Fraser?"

Bajadas frowned. "Perhaps. Ask him yourself tonight at dinner—if he is in a good enough mood."

At the marina basin, Bajadas went over to an elderly watchman sitting outside a hut, spoke to him, and came back tossing a key in the palm of one hand. Then he led the way out along the concrete pier and over the pontoons, past the other moored craft, to the *Black Bear*.

Tugging listlessly at her lines, the white sloop looked shabbier than ever in the bright sunlight. But Gaunt could imagine her spruced up and under sail, white water chuckling from her bows. He could understand how she could stir a man's pride—particularly a man with no other ties, as Peter Fraser had been.

Though more and more the picture he was building of Fraser was a strange amalgam of good and bad, of strangeness and uncertainty.

"Señor Gaunt." Bajadas had crossed to the sloop's deck and was waiting. "If you're ready; I haven't much time."

He nodded and crossed over. They reached the cockpit, where the small steering-wheel twitched idly against its lashing, and Bajadas fitted the key into the hatchway door which led to the cabin space. Then he stopped and frowned. A small dinghy with a tiny, rasping outboard engine was steering in towards them, Marta Weber small and confident at the tiller, the great bulk of her dog sprawled comfortably at the gunwale, his head staring down at the water.

"*Hola.*" She grinned at them and spun the dinghy round. "Since when did you know about boats, Milo?"

"I know enough." He scowled at her. "Why aren't you at school?"

"I had a headache again, so I went swimming instead," she called back, and winked. "What are you doing?"

"Nothing that is your business," said Bajadas impatiently.

"*Gracias*, Milo." She held the dinghy close to the *Black Bear*'s stern and mocked him with a grin. Then she switched her attention to Gaunt. "Do you like swimming, señor—for real, in the sea? I could show you some good places to try."

"I don't swim," lied Gaunt, thinking of the bruises beneath his shirt. But the boat, with its puttering engine, sparked an idea. "How about taking me a trip round the bay, Marta?"

"Okay." She nodded cheerfully. "I'll be back."

As the little boat curved away, Bajadas unlocked the hatchway door, opened it, then led the way down the short flight of steps to the main cabin. Gaunt followed him, the smell of stable bilges and general damp hitting his nostrils as he looked around in the light coming in through the few small windows.

It was a compact layout, saloon berth couches running along each side, a small galley installed to starboard, the broad stem of the aluminium mast like a centre-piece to it all, the sole of the mast resting on a metal plate sunk into the cabin deck. Nearer the bow, behind a light screen door, the sloop's builders had fitted a complete shower and toilet unit. Aft, squeezing along a narrow companion-way, Gaunt glanced at the neatly installed diesel unit. Beside it, tools hung in position on a rack and an open locker was stocked with a variety of spares.

Bajadas had been following him, always close at his heels, saying nothing. Gaunt waited until they were back in the main cabin again.

"She's in reasonable shape," he said casually. "How much had to be fixed after the local pirates broke in?"

"That?" Bajadas swallowed and gave a dismissive gesture. "Only a few things. There are always thieves, Señor Gaunt; lockers were emptied, they searched around for valuables."

Gaunt stooped and fingered a long, repaired cut which ran along the fabric edge of one of the couches.

"They certainly tried," he said drily.

"*Sí.*" Bajadas moistened his lips. "It was unfortunate."

"That's a good word," agreed Gaunt.

They went back up into the cockpit and Bajadas carefully locked the hatchway door again, then glanced at his watch.

"I have to keep that appointment," he said. "If you are having lunch at the hotel, I should be at our sales office by then."

"I'll look in, sometime," promised Gaunt. He leaned back against the cockpit rail, hands in his trouser pockets. "But maybe not for lunch; I found a bar I liked in the old village last night. I'll maybe try it again."

Bajadas frowned but showed no surprise. Nodding, he made his way across the deck to the pontoon, then set off along the pier at a rapid walk.

Gaunt stayed in the cockpit, the heat of the sun soaking into him, glad of a few moments to himself. A big, solitary gull came planing in, circled the mast-head, landed on the sloop's deck, then saw him and took off again in a noisy flapping of wings. One of the yachts at the next pontoon, slightly smaller than the *Black Bear* and with a bright blue hull, was heading out to sea and he watched the brief bustle aboard as she cleared her mooring and her sails began to shiver in the light wind.

As the yacht moved out, he saw Marta's dinghy returning. His mouth tightened. She was very young, totally innocent, and he was using her in a way that he hated. Paul Weber was her stepbrother, she could be badly hurt if things went the way he planned.

But he had to balance against that all the other things which had happened, the deaths, the bitter memory of Lorna Tabor in a hospital bed. He couldn't afford the luxury of choice, he had to use whatever means came his way.

He waved a greeting as the dinghy came puttering in. It bumped lightly against the *Black Bear*'s hull and he climbed down and settled in the centre thwart.

"What would you like to see?" asked Marta.

"The lot." He gestured vaguely at the bay. "How about the north side first?"

"That's what I'd choose." She opened the outboard's throttle and swung the tiller. "When did Milo leave?"

"A few minutes ago." He leaned forward, stroked the dog, and was rewarded with a muted rumble of approval.

"I know what's wrong with Milo." Marta concentrated on the

boat's heading for a moment. "One of the site foremen is off sick; he was in a fight last night. Milo had to get his shoes dirty, sorting things out; he doesn't like that."

"I can imagine." Gaunt had his own idea what had happened to the sick foreman. He watched as they neared the breakwater then rounded it, the dinghy starting a gentle, regular pitching as it met the low swell of the open sea. "Who taught you to handle a boat—Peter Fraser?"

"Who else?" The youngster looked surprised. "It wasn't Milo—or Paul."

He nodded. "How do you get on with Paul?"

"This is *prohibido*, that is *prohibido*—" She grimaced. "All right, I suppose. Mostly, he ignores me."

Gaunt left it at that and the little boat throbbed on, nosing along the north side of the bay, close under the towering cliffs.

The sea was deep and clear, dappled by underwater patches of dark, wavering weed. Fish of all sizes and colouration darted below the boat, an occasional inquisitive sea-bird hovered overhead, and his young boat-handler was content to steer, point out an occasional landmark, and sometimes sing to herself. Then, at last, they turned and with the tide pushing behind them they swept on a new course towards the other side of the bay.

There was shoal rock on that side of the bay, and they stayed farther out. But as they drew level with the dark green slopes of Paul Weber's banana plantation Gaunt considered it closely.

He could see the high wire fence that ran unbroken down to the foreshore and into the sea on either side. There was more shoal rock there, but a landing might be possible for something the size of their dinghy. Beyond the shore there was an area of scrub and loose rock, then the first terraces of the plantation began and went on from there—row upon row of the strange rhizome plants, the distinctive Canary Isles dwarf variety, barely the height of a man, most of them heavily laden with green fruit.

"Bananas." Marta shaped a rude loud noise with her lips. "Paul will be up there somewhere, counting them like money. I hate bananas."

She swung the tiller hard over as she spoke. The dinghy lurched, a stray wave slapped its side, and a fine curtain of spray drenched over everything. At the bow, Oro scrambled into a more secure position and shook himself dry.

"What's wrong with bananas?" asked Gaunt.

"They make me throw up," she said with a scowl. "I wouldn't go near his plantation, even if he allowed me in there."

"Why won't he?"

"How would I know? I'm not supposed to know anything." She slammed the throttle wide open, and the dinghy began slapping through the waves.

They were back in the marina, the dinghy tied to a mooring line and Oro already bounding along the pier, before he asked her anything else.

"Remember telling me last night about that storm?" Gaunt steadied the boat, let her scramble out, then followed. "Did Peter Fraser ever talk about it afterwards?"

"Sometimes, sí." Marta gave him a puzzled look.

"Did he promise you anything as a present, a way to remember what happened?"

She frowned at him in a way that was older than her years. "Why?"

Gaunt shrugged. "People sometimes do, when they've shared something together—the way you did."

"He gave me a gold pendant, for my birthday." She hesitated.

"Nothing else?" asked Gaunt softly.

"It was to be a secret." She eyed him uncertainly. "Something for when I was older. But he only talked about it once, Señor Gaunt. Then I think he forgot; he didn't talk about it again."

"Do you know what it was going to be?"

She shook her head. "He didn't tell me."

"Maybe he forgot," agreed Gaunt, disappointed. He ruffled her hair. "Thanks for the trip, Marta."

She grinned, gave a chirping whistle which brought Oro running, and they went off together.

First, he paid a brief visit to the apartment block and left his brief-case in a drawer in the bedroom. Then, outside again, he waved down a taxi which had just dropped passengers at the Hotel Agosto and told the driver to take him to the old village.

It was a short ride. He paid off the driver with a tip almost as big as the fare and went into the Bar Tomás. The time was only a few minutes after noon and the little tin-roofed bar was deserted, buzzing with flies. Gaunt settled on one of the plain wooden stools at the bar counter and after a few moments the fat elderly figure of Tomás Reales emerged from behind a curtain at the rear.

"*Buenos tardes, señor.*" He waddled over, his round face empty of expression. "So you came back."

"I like your architecture," Gaunt reminded him. "And you look after your customers."

"Sometimes." Reales put a glass in front of him, produced a bottle from under the counter, and poured a measure of pale yellow liquid. "*Licor de banana;* my son thought you might like to try it."

Gaunt sipped. The banana-based liqueur was fiery but sweet.

"Is Miguel here?" he asked.

"*Sí.*" The bar owner frowned a little. "But I want him in no trouble with the law, señor."

"It'll be that way," Gaunt assured him.

Reales looked at him for a moment, then wiped the counter top with a cloth.

"We have a good bean soup, and chicken stew," he said.

Gaunt nodded, and the man ambled through to the kitchen area. He heard a low murmur of voices and a clash of dishes, then Miguel Reales appeared, grinning, wearing a fancy embroidered white shirt, and carrying two earthenware bowls and some basic cutlery.

"Yours, Señor Gaunt." He set the bowls down with a flourish, then leaned his elbows on the counter. "Do you need me for something special?"

"That's the general idea." Gaunt eyed the shirt. "How much was in that wallet last night?"

"Enough." Miguel winked. "But should you have come here like this? Suppose someone else is watching you."

"I told them where I'd be," said Gaunt. "Any salt?"

A salt-cellar was pushed towards him. Miguel waited patiently while he used it and took a first mouthful of soup.

"The Weber plantation," said Gaunt. "How do you feel about going back there, taking me with you?"

Miguel's grin faded. He eased back from the counter and stood fingering his gold ear-ring, saying nothing.

"We'd go in from the sea," Gaunt told him.

"The rocks—" began Miguel.

"If they worry you, maybe your father could do it," said Gaunt sarcastically.

Miguel swore under his breath.

"First, I would have to steal a boat; there are fewer questions that way," he said wearily. "When?"

"Tonight, late."

The young islander moistened his lips.

"It would give you a chance to get even for those stripes on your back," said Gaunt. He stirred the soup in front of him, conscious that Miguel was staring. "I'm here to do a job, Miguel—with or without you."

"Weber?"

He nodded.

"Are you policía?"

"No. But you'd be on the right side of the law—unless we were caught."

"Tonight then," said Miguel Reales softly. "There is an old jetty just along the shore from here. I'll be there from midnight."

"Not in that shirt," warned Gaunt.

"I'll wear my thieving clothes," promised Miguel.

He went off, chuckling.

A few customers had drifted in by the time Gaunt finished eating. Placing some money on the bar counter, he left and spent a little time exploring more of the old village. Going into a small hardware-shop, he bought a simple hand-fishing line with a wooden cross-piece, twin barbed hooks, and a heavy lead sinker. He had them in a plastic bag when he walked back to the tourist strip through the heat of the afternoon.

Most of the Hotel Agosto's guests seemed to have opted for a sun-tanning session. The pool area offered a display of flesh from partly cooked onward, and the smell of sun-tan oil hung like a cloud in the air. Chairs and loungers were filled, some late comers had to be content with a towel spread on the oven-like tiles.

Feeling overdressed, the plastic bag swinging at his side, Gaunt threaded his way through the sun-worshippers. He spotted Hannah North as she emerged from the pool beside a tall, deeply tanned man who had dark hair, a small moustache, and the physique of a lean fighting bull.

He knew he was staring, but Hannah was magnificent in a dark brown two piece swim-suit. From the way the fighting bull hovered, draping a towel around her shoulders, he thought the same.

Gaunt caught her eye, turned and went to a pool-side kiosk under a brightly coloured awning. He bought an iced lemonade and stood sipping it in the shade; after a minute Hannah came up to the counter.

"We have to talk," murmured Gaunt, the lemonade almost at his lips.

"That doesn't make my day." She opened her purse and paid for a pack of English cigarettes. "I'm Room 720. Go up now, I'll follow —and we'll have company."

Leaving, she brushed against him and Gaunt was left with her room key in his hand.

If he was still being followed it didn't seem to apply inside the hotel. But he was careful, left the elevator at the fifth floor, and walked up the remaining two floors. The corridor was empty as he used Hannah's key and slipped into her room.

The room had a view across the bay and a large double bed. Underwear was draped over a chair and any one of the perfumes on the dressing table would have cost a small ransom in any Edinburgh shop. He flopped down on the bed, lay back with his hands behind his head, and waited.

It was several minutes before the door swung open. Hannah came in, wearing a beach-robe. The fighting bull padded behind her looking healthier than ever, dressed in a towelling shirt and a pair of khaki shorts.

"Get off my bed," said Hannah coldly. She indicated her companion. "Captain Farise is from the Governor-General's office; he's our contact."

"Roberto Farise—Bobi to my friends, Señor Gaunt," said Farise. He spoke English with a faint American accent and, once Gaunt was off the bed, he shook hands with a crushing enthusiasm. "Hannah has told me about you."

"That helps." Gaunt hoped it did. "How does the Governor-General's office fit in?"

"Simply." Farise broke off and fussed Hannah into a chair. She looked pleased and didn't object. "Originally I was police, in Spain, then Ministry of Justice. Now I am on staff out here to deal with problem situations."

"Like getting rid of a magistrate," murmured Hannah. She saw Gaunt's raised eyebrow and nodded. "Señor Martinez will be kept busy until late tomorrow; we can forget about him."

"Thanks." Gaunt sat on the edge of the bed again and ignored her glare. "How about you, Hannah? Did you do the apartment tour?"

"With your long-haired friend Bajadas, who has wandering hands," she said grimly. "The apartments are interesting, but I could have done without him. Are you still seeing Weber tonight?"

"Eating with him; he'll know by then about the sale postponement." Gaunt shrugged and looked at Captain Farise. "Are you keeping any kind of tag on me, Bobi?"

"Not yet," said Farise seriously. "I thought about it, till Hannah said to leave you on your own. But if you want—"

"No." Gaunt shook his head firmly. "And not tonight. Weber has a banana plantation where he doesn't like visitors. I'd like to find out why."

Farise sighed. "You realise this man has broken no law we know about, that he has prominent friends, is of good commercial standing?"

"Does that make a difference?" asked Gaunt.

"Hell, no." Farise looked shocked. "Just don't tell me too much."

Hannah's beach-robe had fallen open. She sat with one arm along the back of her chair, frowning.

"What about the child?" she asked.

"I tried again. No luck," said Gaunt shortly.

Hannah looked thoughtful.

"Suppose the original of that old Fraser company share certificate turns up, gifted to her? What happens?"

Gaunt shrugged. "The Mills of God may grind slow, but they're like greased lightning compared with the law courts—and cost a lot less. If she was lucky, she might get some of the cash as an old-age pension." He drew a deep breath. "Heard anything from Edinburgh yet?"

"Henry called before lunch." Hannah North saw the question in his eyes and shook her head. "Nothing fresh, Jonny. Lorna Tabor's condition hasn't changed."

"It could take time." Gaunt wondered who he was trying to convince. Getting to his feet, he picked up the plastic bag. "Hannah, unless there's another problem I'll leave contacting you till after I've been in that plantation." He turned to Farise. "Can you stay available?"

"Of course." Farise gave a sideways glance at Hannah and rubbed a finger along his dark moustache. "You can rely on it."

"What about right now?" asked Hannah, frowning. "What are you going to do? We should know."

"I'm going fishing." Gaunt gave them a lopsided grin. "It beats thinking any day."

Finding some bait wasn't difficult. There were half a dozen amateur fishermen already trying their luck at different locations along the marina breakwater, and he scrounged what he needed.

Gaunt sat in a patch of shade, his back against a concrete block, and let his line drift and swirl on a tiny, bobbing float.

He'd partly lied to Hannah and Captain Farise. He needed a chance to think, to attempt to weave possibilities across the gaps in the little he knew. He could look across the marina and see the *Black Bear* at her pontoon berth. Whatever her secret, there was nothing he could do about it, short of having her literally taken to bits in some boat-yard.

So it came back to Paul Weber and his Hispan Trading, and the real operation going on behind that flimsy screen. Drugs, gun-running—he tried to build up a mental list but knew he was fooling himself, making a pretence of doing something useful.

The float quivered and jerked. He hauled in a small, brightly striped fish, put fresh bait on the hook, and let the line drift out again. He watched it pensively. Going to the banana plantation would be a different kind of fishing expedition.

The kind that could turn out to be nasty and dangerous.

He stayed out on the breakwater until after six, when the air began to cool. By then, he had caught a handful of the same small fish but he gave them to one of the other anglers as he left. On the way out, he discovered he had a new shadow. A young man with dark sun-glasses and a blue sports shirt stopped leaning against a wall and made a clumsy attempt to be inconspicuous as he trailed behind.

Back in the apartment, Gaunt helped himself to a beer and took it out on to the balcony. Blue Shirt and Sun-glasses was leaning against a parked car on the other side of the road, looking totally bored.

But he was there. Gaunt went inside again and closed the veranda window.

Paul Weber's dinner invitation had been for eight. The same white Mercedes with sheepskin seat-covers arrived outside the El Barco apartments a few minutes before eight and Milo Bajadas, immaculate in a red shirt and white linen suit, climbed the stairs to collect Gaunt.

Gaunt finished the knot in his tie and picked up his jacket. He had showered and wore a clean white shirt with his only suit. For some crazy, obtuse reason, the only time it had ever happened to him, he wanted to go along with the formalities, at least look the part of a British civil servant.

"You told Weber about the *Black Bear* situation?"

Bajadas nodded gloomily at the memory.

"He wasn't happy." His voice made it a sad understatement. "But he accepts you can't be blamed."

"A reasonable man," said Gaunt cheerfully.

The sarcasm was lost. Bajadas led the way down to the Mercedes and they set off on the short drive.

There were other cars, some big, all expensive, in the driveway outside the Villa Hispan. Gaunt glanced at Bajadas, and Weber's personal assistant gave a shrug.

"One or two of Paul's friends are looking in for a drink." He produced a comb and gave his long, black hair a quick tidy. "It was meant to be a small celebration."

A maid answered the doorbell, then Bajadas led the way into a large reception room. It had red velvet curtains, silver glinted on the sideboards, and a dozen or so guests stood talking, glasses in their hands. Paul Weber left one couple and came over. He wore a light-weight dark blue stockbroker suit. His heavy features forced what was meant to be a smile.

"Sorry about today," said Gaunt.

"Bureaucracy." Weber made the word sound unclean. "I called Santa Cruz and got hold of Martínez—our magistrate. He's sitting around, twiddling his thumbs." For a moment the man's sharp eyes considered Gaunt with a degree of suspicion. "He'll be back to-morrow."

"And that'll be everything," said Gaunt. He faked a sigh. "It's going to cut into my plans. I'd hoped to squeeze enough free time to see more of the island."

"We'll manage something for you—after I've got the boat." Weber beckoned another maid, circulating with a drinks tray, and waited until Gaunt had a glass. "I'll introduce you around."

He did. Two were local landowners, each with an overdressed wife. Then came a politician, another man, grossly overweight, was an industrialist from Madrid who had a villa near the village. Names, smiles and handshakes round the room took a few minutes. Then Weber muttered an apology and abandoned him.

Gaunt sipped his drink, a rum-based cocktail, then felt a hand tug at his arm. He turned, then grinned.

"Hi, Marta."

"*Buenas tardes*, Jonny." The child smiled up at him. It was the first time he'd seen her wearing a dress, a dark green cotton print with a piping of white lace at the neck and sleeves. Her hair had been brushed back, and her eyes sparkled. "Do I look good?"

"Good enough to be a princess," he said positively. He noticed the gold pendant round her neck, on a narrow gold chain. "Your pendant—is that the one you told me about, the one you got from Peter Fraser?"

She nodded. "He said it came from New York."

"Can I see?" He took the pendant in his fingers. The face was a small, cameo-like miniature of a sailing boat, and when he turned it over the other side was plain except for a hallmark and, beside it, in tiny letters, the one word "Tiffany." He pursed his lips appreciatively. "He was right: New York is where it came from."

"I think I'll go there when I'm older," said Marta seriously. "To see everything—not to live there."

"Do that." Gaunt frowned. "Where's your hairy monster?"

"Oro? He's locked in the kitchen."

"He probably wouldn't like it much here," said Gaunt. "No decent dog would. Where did you learn that way of whistling him in?"

She shrugged. "On Gomera. Oro was born over there. On Gomera—"

"People whistle," Gaunt agreed. "I was in a bar in the old village. The owner told me."

"Tomás Reales?" Marta laughed. "I know him, and his son." She looked around, as if to make sure Weber wasn't in sight. "Paul wouldn't like that."

"I won't tell him," promised Gaunt.

She grimaced. "I keep Oro away from Paul. He'd like to get rid of Oro, but my father gave me him—"

"So he can't do much about it," Gaunt nodded.

Someone else called Marta by name. She smiled and went away. Briefly, he was caught by one of the landowners. Then Weber returned—and Gaunt stared at the tall, thin figure, who was with his host.

"Hello, Gaunt," said John Cass. His small mouth shaped a smirking smile. "Paul thought you'd be surprised."

"It happens all the time," agreed Gaunt. "When did you get in?"

"To Tenerife?" The Hispan manager rubbed a finger down the side of his beaked nose, a gesture Gaunt remembered only too well. "This morning."

"Overnight from Paris," said Weber. "John had to go over there to chase an order."

"Which he didn't get." Cass gestured sadly with his hands. "But some other things look brighter; that's why I'm here." He frowned at Gaunt. "You know, I tried to see you again, back in Edinburgh—about that Anderson woman business. But you were out each time."

"Tidying it up," lied Gaunt convincingly. He grinned at Weber.

"Then tomorrow, when I get a last piece of paper sorted out, everyone will be happy."

Weber nodded, but was glaring just past him. Puzzled, Gaunt turned and saw Marta standing behind him.

"Marta." Weber's voice was low and angry. "I've told you before. Stop hanging around when I'm talking business."

"Paul, I wasn't." The child's face flushed with embarrassment. "I—"

"Don't argue," snapped Weber. "Get out of here."

"But Paul—" she protested.

Weber took one step forward and slapped her hard across the cheek. Marta stared at him but didn't utter a sound, and Weber's hand rose again. Gaunt froze, willing himself to do nothing, fighting down an urge to block what was coming.

But conversation had died all around, and Weber's guests were staring. The man swallowed, lowered his hand, turned his back on Marta, and walked over to the window. She looked after him for a moment, then slowly, defiantly, she left the room. Gradually, conversation picked up again.

"How'd you like to have to work for him, Gaunt?" murmured John Cass, his thin face showing a faint, cold amusement. "It can be rough. Think your nice, genteel government service training could cope?"

"We'd cope." Gaunt considered the thick-set figure, who had left the window and was mingling with his guests again, laughing at a joke one was telling. "All things nasty can come our way."

Cass stiffened and changed the subject.

The cocktail party dragged on for another half hour; then as dusk gave way to darkness the guests departed. Weber saw them off and returned in an affable mood as the last car drove away.

"It's time we ate." He touched Gaunt's arm. "Let's go through. Cass is joining us, but I promise neither of us will talk shop."

The villa's dining-room housed a vast mahogany table which could have held a dozen without being crowded. But a smaller table had been set beside it and a grey-haired manservant saw them seated, then, helped by one of the maids, served the meal.

Paul Weber's hospitality couldn't be faulted. A starter of shrimps was followed by thinly sliced tender pork, served with a hot pepper sauce. That was followed in turn by a nougat sweet and goat's cheese. Only one wine, a dry muscatel, was served throughout.

Gaunt sipped it sparingly and was glad. Gradually, never seeming to push, Weber brought the conversation round first to the Remembrancer's Office and then from there, smoothly and naturally, to what had happened to Peter Fraser's estate.

As if on cue, John Cass took it up from there.

"You had Mrs. Anderson first—your Canadian connection," he said. "Then after she died, the other woman from Canada. I didn't meet her. What's she like?"

"Younger, pleasant." Gaunt thought of Lorna Tabor and what had happened to her.

"Genuine?"

"Probably."

"So by your rules, she may inherit—inherit anything that belonged to Fraser?" asked Weber bluntly.

"It's not quite that simple." Deliberately, Gaunt launched into a long, droning account of the Queen's Bounty procedure and ignored Weber's gathering impatience. "We have to be thorough."

"It shows," said Weber with a thinly veiled sarcasm.

They tried him again, when the manservant brought brandy in fine crystal glasses. Each time an apparently innocent question led to another, a probing process when he could easily have said the wrong thing and exposed the turmoil back in Edinburgh. But Gaunt won through and, at last, Weber gave up. Wiping his mouth on his napkin, he looked at his wrist-watch.

"It's getting late. Cass and I have some business to sort out: he's flying back tomorrow." He gave a grunt and pushed back his chair. "As soon as the *Black Bear* papers are cleared—"

"I'll bring them to you," promised Gaunt, pushing back his chair.

Bajadas drove him back to the apartment, said goodnight as Gaunt got out, then drove off. There was a small Seat coupe parked further along the street and the man lounging behind the wheel shrank down as the Mercedes' headlights swept across it.

Gaunt climbed the stairs and went into the apartment. He locked the door, closed the curtains on the veranda window, and checked the time. He had almost an hour.

He waited another twenty minutes, then changed his suit for a dark sweater and slacks. Unscrewing the ventilator in the shower-room, he brought out the cardboard box marked "Accessories," opened it, and hefted each of the two pear-shaped blast grenades. They had belt clips attached, but he put the grenades in the plastic bag beside the fishing-line. They were insurance, nothing more.

Switching off the apartment lights, he left by the rear window and made his way up to the top of the rocky slope. Then, keeping low, he looked down. The same Seat car was still parked below, without lights.

The top of the slope was unexplored territory but there was enough moonlight to guide his way. Once he had gone through the trees, there was a narrow track. From there, keeping well clear of the bright lights of the tourist strip, he made his way to the old village and struck down a lane to the shore.

The jetty lay ahead, a dilapidated timber walkway running out into the water. It looked deserted, but as he reached it Miguel Reales stepped out of the shadows.

"*Hola.*" Miguel grinned at him in the darkness. He was wearing a black sweater and dungaree trousers, and a knife was tucked into the broad leather belt at his waist. "We have your boat, Señor Gaunt."

"We?" Gaunt frowned at him.

Miguel beckoned.

The boat, a neat rubber inflatable, was floating under the jetty. Someone else was already aboard, holding it steady against the timbers. Miguel nodded and they scrambled down. Gaunt settled in the dinghy, then swore under his breath as he saw who he was facing.

"Tomás"—he stared at the fat, elderly bar owner, then swung round as Miguel joined them—"what the hell's he doing here?"

"My father is an old fool," said Miguel. "He wanted to come." Then he gave a mock sigh which held more than a hint of pride. "But the same old fool handles a boat better than I can. So—"

Gaunt nodded, leaned forward, and gripped Tomás's shoulder in a silent thanks. Father and son exchanged a wink, each took up a stubby, broad-bladed oar, and they pulled out into the low swell.

CHAPTER SEVEN

A light swell was running, Tomás and Miguel Reales plied their oars in a measured, economical rhythm, and Jonathan Gaunt was content to leave them to it.

Initially, their course was out towards the middle of the bay while the lights of Puerto Tellas shrank behind them. Then Tomás grunted, the small, broad-bladed oars dipped in a different rhythm, and the inflatable swung round. They had begun the second half of a dogleg approach to the plantation shore line.

The land ahead was a stark black outline in the night, an outline edged by milky broken water churning in over shoal rock. They came nearer, the broken water became separate patterns of white surf, and the murmur of the sea began to grow.

Tomás grunted again. Suddenly the older man had shuffled round in the boat, facing the bow, now with both oars and using them sparingly.

They went in, and the inflatable was suddenly pitching in the lumping water. Her rubber hull grazed an unseen rock and she lurched briefly, began to spin, then steadied as Tomás hauled on one oar. Another line of white came up, they rounded it, then angled between two more while the bulky figure worked unemotionally at the oars.

Then, equally suddenly, they were through. The inflatable grounded on loose shingle, they stepped out into a few inches of foaming water, and another minute was enough to drag the little boat clear across dry shingle and into the shelter of an outcrop of rock.

A cricket was chirping above the sound of the sea, hidden somewhere near. A small unseen shape rustled off through the coarse, dry stunted grass where the shingle ended. Beyond the grass was a rising maze of low scrubland and above that, Gaunt could see the first, dark solid rows of banana plants.

Miguel and his father were muttering behind him, their voices low. He waited, taking the two grenades from their plastic bag and clipping them to his belt, then turned and glanced round as the muttering kept on. It sounded angry on both sides, it lasted another few seconds, then Miguel came over, alone.

"What was that about?" asked Gaunt.

"The old fool wanted to come with us," scowled Miguel. "I told him he had agreed: he would stay with the boat."

"Is it settled?"

Nodding, Miguel reached into a pocket and produced two black cloth hoods. They had eye-slits cut in them.

"Wear this, *por favor,*" he said, handing one to Gaunt.

As he did, he saw the grenades. His mouth opened, then he quickly closed it again, saying nothing. Gaunt pulled on the hood. The eye-slits were adequate, he ignored the rank, stale smell of the material.

"Ready, señor?" asked Miguel.

Gaunt glanced back at Tomás, standing scowling beside the boat, then nodded. Miguel in the lead, they set off.

A low drystone wall marked the plantation's boundary line but there was no other barrier. Once over the wall, they were in among chest-high, thick-stemmed banana plants, broad leaves brushing at their clothes, the heavy, close-packed stalk of bananas on each clearly visible.

"A good crop," murmured Miguel. He chuckled under his breath. "But you want to find what else grows here, eh?"

They plodded on through the rows, then reached a rutted track and turned left, following it up the slope but staying near the edge, close to cover.

The track took a bend and, suddenly, Miguel came to a halt, then pointed. The dark, low silhouette of the plantation office showed in a clearing ahead, a light behind one window, a Jeep parked outside. They moved closer. The single-storey brick structure was larger than Gaunt had expected. A power line ran on poles to a transformer box beside it, but Gaunt could only see one door, close to the lighted window.

"Any other way in and out?" he asked softly.

Miguel shook his head. "Only to a store-room, Señor Gaunt. I discovered that last time."

"Then we'd better find out the rest of it," said Gaunt.

They went forward again, moving silently, the last short distance the worst, with no possible cover. But then they were at the Jeep and from there Gaunt crept to the lighted window. Hugging the cool brick of the wall, he risked a quick glance inside, then pulled back quickly.

The two men in the room were burly and unshaven, both wearing denims and heavy boots. One had his feet up on a desk and was reading a magazine. The other was listening to a transistor radio, using an ear-piece. There were flasks of coffee and an opened pack of sandwiches beside them.

There was also a double-barrelled shotgun.

He eased back to where Miguel was waiting.

"How many?" hissed Miguel through the black hood.

"Two."

Squatting down for a moment, Gaunt considered the options. He felt a tap on his shoulder, and Miguel was pointing hopefully to the grenades.

"Don't be a damned fool," he murmured, and the young islander shrugged apologetically.

There was a less drastic way. He studied the Jeep, grinned to himself, then beckoned and led Miguel a few paces farther away to explain what he wanted. When he understood, Miguel fought down a snort of amusement and nodded enthusiastic agreement.

It meant wriggling into the Jeep, then working in the darkness, touch-tracing the wiring under the dash. The basic business of jumping the ignition leads was simple enough: the army bred some strange, unofficial skills. But the horn relay was chancier and took longer.

At last, Gaunt was ready. He checked that Miguel had melted into the darkness, the way they'd arranged, then he took a deep breath. Twisting his chosen two wires together, he dived out of the Jeep and rolled under as the horn began blaring.

Flattened against the dirt, Gaunt waited. He saw the door of the building swing open and both guards hurry out into the open. One stood gripping the shotgun, the other ran over to the Jeep; then, his booted feet only inches from Gaunt's face, he leaned in and began thumping the horn button, trying to stop the blare. He gave up and shouted and the other man trotted over.

For a moment there were two pairs of booted feet close to his face while the men held a brief, shouted exchange. Then the shotgun was propped against the side of the Jeep, one of the men ambled round to the front of the vehicle, and the hood creaked open.

Gaunt catapulted out, going in a ground-level tackle for the guard still thumping the horn. Surprised, knocked off balance, the man fell hard—and Gaunt kicked the shotgun aside as he pounced on the sprawled, startled figure. There was a flurry of movement at the front of the Jeep, but he ignored it.

The man on the ground recovered fast, tried to struggle upright, and threw a wild punch. Gaunt blocked the blow, slammed an elbow into his opponent's stomach which sent him grunting back, then, both hands together, fingers locked, he landed a chopping blow just behind the guard's ear.

The man collapsed and didn't move. Rolling clear, Gaunt grabbed at the fallen shotgun.

But there was no need. Miguel Reales pocketed his leather cosh and gave a mock salute from the front of the Jeep. The second guard lay on the ground beside him, face-down.

The horn was still blaring. Gaunt broke the wiring connection, then, in the welcome silence, Miguel and Gaunt dragged the two unconscious men over to the office doorway. Miguel found a coil of thin rope in the rear of the Jeep and brought it over.

"Tie them and gag them," said Gaunt. He laid the shotgun against the wall. "Then keep an eye on things out here. Anyone likely to have heard that horn?"

"No one lives near, señor." Miguel shook his head, already using his knife to cut the rope into handy lengths.

Gaunt left him to it and went into the plantation office. The main area was shabby and ordinary with desks and a few filing cabinets. There were some progress charts on the walls. One area, partitioned off, was obviously used by the manager. But there was a door at the rear. It was solid wood, double-locked, and marked "Privado" in bold letters.

A ring of keys was lying on one of the desks the guards had used. He took the ring over, tried the keys one by one, and discovered none fitted. Standing back, he tried an experimental kick and the door didn't budge.

There was only one way left. He went outside, where Miguel had finished dealing with one guard and had started the other. Picking up the shotgun again, Gaunt went back to the double-locked door. Gauging the distance, sighting carefully, he fired one barrel at each lock.

The noise was almost deafening in the confined space. But as the smoke and dust cleared, both locks hung loose. Tossing the empty shotgun aside, he kicked at the door again—and it flew open.

There was a light switch just inside. He flicked it on; neon tubes sputtered to life overhead.

He stared. The room had plain, white-tiled walls and no windows. Down the middle, a small line of office computer equipment sat silent on a desk-height bench with two chairs for operators in front of them. Thick black cables snaked from the bench to a line of grey metal cabinets. A large metal safe was located at the end of the room, where a small table was occupied by an incongruously old-fashioned postal franking machine.

Whatever he'd expected he might find, it hadn't been this. He walked down the length of the bench, identifying a small IBM computer with a linked word processor and two separate printers. Blank v.d.u. screens mocked at him, the safe on the rear wall looked as though nothing short of a shaped explosive charge or a thermal lance would make any impression on it.

He tried one of the keyboards, but wherever the main power source was located, it was off. Swearing under his breath, he leaned his knuckles on the metal bench and looked around again.

This was the place that mattered. There had to be something, somewhere.

There was a waste bucket. He emptied it on the floor and salvaged a crumpled section of torn print-out paper, perhaps the start of a trial run. Smoothing it out, he saw it was an account form, made out to a London firm for an entry in a trade directory, the amount due—four hundred pounds sterling, payment requested by return.

But the letterhead address at the top was a publishing house in Barcelona, and payment was to be made direct to an English address in Liverpool.

He rummaged through the rest of the waste bucket's contents, then went from there to the franking machine. On some separate circuit, the machine worked when he switched on and he fed a scrap of paper through it.

The postal franking was Spanish, but the postmark was a hazy blur.

None of it made sense. None of it, unless—He stared at the scrap of franked paper in his one hand and the salvaged computer-printed invoice in the other, with a dawning understanding.

If he was right, Paul Weber certainly had something to hide, something to worry about—and if he had to buy the *Black Bear* to protect it, then the money involved probably rated as petty cash.

He went back to the bench, ripped away the plastic guards protecting the paper feed trays on both printers, and tore off a sample from each roll. They were totally different in layout and in letterhead addresses. But both were invoice forms for trade directories—dull, unexciting in appearance.

Yet if he was right, and he had to be right—

"Señor Gaunt—"

Miguel's agitated voice jerked him round. The islander was standing by the shattered door, his hood removed, his face tense.

"What's wrong?"

"My father says—"

"Your father—" Gaunt blinked.

"He followed us. He's watching the track—somewhere farther along, nearer the road." Miguel moistened his lips. "He called to me, our way—whistling, you understand? A car is coming, is through the gates—"

"Heading here?" Cursing under his breath, Gaunt stuffed the sheets of paper into a pocket. "All right, I'm finished." He stopped short and almost groaned at his own stupidity.

Close to where Miguel was standing a small box was set into the tiled wall. Another small, identical box was on the opposite wall. When he'd barged into the inner room, he'd broken an electronic beam alarm.

Paul Weber didn't rely totally on the human element.

"Señor—" pleaded Miguel.

He nodded and they hurried together through the main office area and out the main door, past where Weber's two guards were lying trussed. A chirping whistle sounded in the darkness. Miguel gave a short, shrill reply, then grabbed Gaunt's arm as a pair of headlights swept round a bend in the track, wavering, coming nearer as they watched.

"Move. Head back to the boat." Gaunt shoved him on his way, watching the headlights, hearing the car's engine bellow as the driver thrashed it along the rough track.

The headlights swept round a final bend, bathing the office block in light—and catching Miguel, almost at the start of the banana plants.

Blast grenades had a standard ten-second fuse. Praying they hadn't been altered, Gaunt grabbed one grenade from his belt, pulled the pin release, and lobbed the grenade into the front seat of the parked Jeep.

Sprinting away, heading for the plantation, not looking back, he heard the car behind him skid to a halt. Doors opened, a man shouted, a handgun barked.

Then the Jeep blew up as the grenade exploded. He felt the blast on his back and almost fell, his ears sang as he stumbled on, and a second explosion, the Jeep's fuel tank going up, followed a moment later.

He reached the start of the banana lines, dived into shelter, then glanced back. Flames rose from the shattered wreck of the Jeep, two men were helping another to his feet, a fourth was crawling towards the car, and old Seat station wagon.

It was no time to linger. Turning, Gaunt plunged deeper into the safety of the tall leafy stems.

Twice he heard shouts, then shots. Tripping, falling, losing his sense of direction more than once, the glow behind him which marked the burning Jeep fading and ending, he forced himself on.

At last, he reached the shore. No sounds of pursuit reached his ears and he finally located the rock where the rubber boat lay waiting. Weary, his back aching, a pain stabbing in his ribs to remind him he was a fool, he pulled off the stinking black hood, slumped down against the rock and rested.

It was a long time before Miguel and his father appeared, walking slowly along the shingle. Miguel was half supporting Tomás Reales and when they reached Gaunt the older man was swaying, almost ready to collapse. His right arm was hanging limp, the faint moonlight showed his shoulder was sticky with blood.

"I found him," said Miguel tiredly. He anticipated Gaunt's question. "They were firing at shadows; he was just unlucky."

"I'm sorry." Gaunt chewed his lip. "Any of them coming this way?"

"None. They search back towards the road." Miguel paused as his father muttered to him, then twisted a grin. "He says it isn't a bad wound. He has been hurt more opening a bottle."

"Once he's fixed, I'll open a bottle for both of you, as a starter," promised Gaunt grimly.

They left Tomás propped against the rock and dragged the inflatable down to the water's edge. Then, going back, they collected the older man and helped him aboard. Wading out into the surf, they pushed the inflatable clear, then scrambled in and took the oars. The white hazards of the shoal reefs came up but, croaking instructions from the stern, gesturing furiously with his good arm, Tomás safely piloted them through.

Then, once they were clear, he was content to lie back and leave the long, dogleg pull across the bay to Gaunt and his son. He didn't stir until, nosing in through the darkness, they bumped the jetty at the old village.

The boat secured, Gaunt helped Miguel bring his father ashore. "*Gracias.* I'll manage now." Miguel muttered an apology as he got an arm around his father and elbowed Gaunt in the process. "We have friends close by, we know a *médico*—"

"I'll stay with you," volunteered Gaunt.

"No, Señor Gaunt." Miguel was polite but firm. "Go your own way."

"*Sí*, it would be better," said Tomás weakly, nodding. "Tell me one thing. Did—did you get what you wanted?"

"I think so," said Gaunt quietly.

Tomás forced a grin and grunted to his son, and, one supporting the other, they left him.

It was after 2 A.M., the narrow streets were dark and deserted, and even what Gaunt could see of the tourist strip had died till morning. But he needed his own kind of help now, and urgently.

There was a public telephone stand at the next street corner. He fed some coins into its slot, dialled the Hotel Agosto, and asked the night operator for Hannah North's room. When she answered and heard his voice, Hannah wasn't pleased.

"It's the middle of the damned night," she protested. "I was asleep. I"—she groaned—"all right, what's happened?"

"A lot, and I'm in trouble," said Gaunt. "I need you, and your Captain Bobi—presuming you've got him handy."

"I'm in bed and I'm alone." Hannah bridled. "If you're insinuating—"

"Hannah, right now I don't care," said Gaunt wearily. "Can you get him?"

"Yes. He's in the hotel; where are you?"

"Hold on." There was a street sign on the nearest house. "Avenida Blanco, in the old village."

"Wait there. He drives a Lancia coupe."

She hung up. Sighing, Gaunt replaced his own receiver, then moved along to a patch of shadow which was a shop doorway. Patting his pockets, he felt the slim outline of the computer prints and let himself relax a little. Then he frowned. Something was missing.

The second grenade; he cursed softly under his breath, knowing it had been clipped to his belt as they rowed back from the plantation, remembering the apparently clumsy way Miguel had collided with him as they came ashore at the jetty.

Miguel was a good thief, too good maybe. The idea of the Reales family having a blast grenade stowed away as a souvenir wasn't one that appealed to him.

But it could wait. Paul Weber was a more immediate concern and a lot more dangerous. By now Weber would know exactly what had happened in the plantation break-in and that the raiders had escaped.

What would Weber do about it, how quickly would he react? In theory, the Hispan boss might still assume he'd had his visitor bottled up in the El Barco apartments. But theory and the way people reacted were two different things, and the name Jonathan Gaunt had to be at the top of Weber's list of suspects.

It was not a happy thought. Gaunt had known it would be that way from the start—and the night felt colder the more he considered it.

The Lancia coupe, big, blood-red and with purring twin exhausts, turned into the Avenida Blanco about ten minutes later. The passenger door swung open and Captain Roberto Farise beckoned impatiently.

"Get in the back," he said curtly. "There's a rug; stay down under it."

Gaunt clambered in behind the unshaven Spaniard, who wore a partly buttoned shirt flapping outside his trousers. As he burrowed under the rug the passenger door slammed shut and the Lancia was moving again.

"Thanks for coming," he said.

"Had I a choice?" asked Farise sarcastically. "Just keep down. I've got to get you into the Agosto and even my humble intelligence tells me you don't want an audience."

The Lancia purred on then, after what seemed only a couple of minutes Gaunt felt the car change gear. They turned and briefly bumped over pot-holes, then the Lancia stopped and the engine stopped.

"All clear," said Farise after a moment. "You can come out."

Gaunt emerged cautiously from the rug and found Farise grinning at him.

"What's so funny?" asked Gaunt.

"Two of us, trying to get into a woman's bedroom in the middle of the night." Farise chuckled. "There may be a few other people tiptoeing between rooms; we mustn't alarm them."

"Just get me there," Gaunt said stonily. "I don't care how."

They were in a lane behind the Agosto, close to the beach, and the hotel was no longer floodlit. Once they'd left the Lancia, they crossed a pitch-black patch of garden and emerged close to the pool area; Farise led the way to a side door.

"Locked from the inside, but I was going out," he murmured,

easing the door open. Once Gaunt had followed him into a dimly lit corridor, he carefully closed and locked the door again. "Now, *por favor,* we should use the service stairs."

They went up, Farise loping ahead up the stairway in a way that left Gaunt cursing. Once they had to stop, hearing voices whispering ahead. But that ended in a giggle and a door slamming, and Farise was off again.

The corridor to Hannah's room was deserted and she opened her door at the first tap. She was in a blouse and slacks, barefooted, but she'd found time and energy to brush her hair and smudge on some lipstick. Waving them in, she closed the door and looked Gaunt up and down.

"You need a drink." She led the way into the room, where the sheets on the bed were still thrown back. Three paper cups were waiting on the bedside table, already filled. "It's brandy—local rotgut."

"Don't despise it," murmured Farise. "What you can't drink is good for clearing drains."

They let Gaunt settle in a chair and watched him take a first gulp of the coarse, dark spirit, and then Farise sucked an edge of his thin moustache for a moment.

"Well?" he asked. "What have you got?"

"These." Gaunt dragged the invoice sheets from his pocket.

"Gracias." Farise took the sheets, raised an eyebrow more than once as he skimmed through their contents, then politely handed them on to Hannah. "And you got these—where?"

"At Weber's plantation."

"Where tonight there was some kind of explosion and some kind of fire. The Guardia Civil were advised it had been a small, unfortunate accident to an electricity transformer," said Farise drily. He gave a slight scowl. "Hannah said trouble; I checked before I came for you. Was anyone killed?"

"I don't think so," said Gaunt carefully.

"Hurt?" Farise sighed when he didn't get an answer. "Hannah was right. Trouble." He gave her one of his admiring, fighting-bull glances. "You should be glad she is here."

"Here for what?" Hannah had finished reading. She slapped the invoice sheets down on her bed. "Suppose someone tells me what the hell is important about these?"

"They prove that Paul Weber is certainly a very rich man," said Farise softly. He paused and gave an odd, almost sympathetic smile. "They also prove that as far as you are concerned, he is a crook."

"How?"

"Ask your friend." Farise made it an invitation, glancing at Gaunt. "How many does he send out?"

"No idea." Gaunt took another anaesthetising swallow of brandy. "Ten thousand a mailing?"

"The last of these I came across was based on Madrid," said Farise. "They ran to one hundred thousand a mailing, expected a ten per cent success rate." He shrugged at Hannah. "That way, they cleared over one million pounds sterling—perhaps three times a year."

"Will both of you stop your damned smirking and tell me?" Her frustration broke through. "You show me a couple of printed invoices, then what? Am I supposed to turn cartwheels? What the hell is Weber doing?"

"It's called fraud," murmured Farise. "He tells a small army of companies that they owe him money; they believe him, and they pay by return."

"Try again," she said incredulously.

"He's right, Hannah," said Gaunt with a degree of sympathy. "The basics are simple. You invent a fake publishing operation, you make out you're going to publish some kind of international directory. Then you bill firms for the amount you say they owe you—"

"And the money rolls in," agreed Farise. He turned to Gaunt. "Have you met this before?"

Gaunt shook his head. "Only heard about it."

"Then you have been lucky, my friend." Farise's tanned handsome face twitched in a grimace. "Before I came to the islands, when I was in Madrid, my department at the Ministry of Justice was involved in one, with Interpol snapping at our heels." He went over to the bed, picked up one of the printed bills, and held it in front of Hannah. "What do you see? A normal, apparently respectable firm sending an account to a client, agreed?"

She nodded, reluctantly.

"Exactly." Farise spoke patiently, as if lecturing a backwards student. "Here we have the Annica International Telex Directory—to be published by Annica, Barcelona. They ask this English firm to pay three hundred and eighty pounds sterling to Annica's account with a branch of a very real English bank. Now, suppose you are the cashier of this English company. Suppose you have different bills and invoices and statements coming in every day—and this one, from Annica, is in a bundle of bills of all kinds. Its looks genuine." He paused and tapped part of the account with a finger. "Here we even have a warning that payment must be made within fifteen days to obtain benefit of a ten per cent discount. So, Hannah, what do you do?"

"I'd check it out," she said stubbornly.

"No." Farise shook his head firmly. "You might, if it was for a much larger sum. But this is small, almost petty cash; you don't want to run to your boss and annoy him."

"You pay it," agreed Gaunt wearily. "That's how it works, Hannah."

"All right." She went over to a cupboard, brought out the brandy bottle, and made a tight-lipped, still not totally convinced business of topping up their paper cups. "But how often?"

"Statistically?" Farise shrugged. "It's guesswork. Between ten and fifteen per cent is the accepted average—not bad, if you sent out a hundred thousand every few months. Then the smart operator makes a special file of the firms who have paid—and they are permanently on his lists. Lists, Hannah—because he operates more than one fake company, more than one nonexistent telex directory."

"And he brings out a new edition each year," said Gaunt. "His customers expect that."

Looking dazed, Hannah took a long swallow of brandy and sat on the edge of her bed.

"You're talking of a gold mine," she said, surrendering.

"How to be a millionaire, in any currency," said Farise. "Jonny, the one you heard about; where was he based?"

"New Zealand." And Scotland, Wales, and most of Ireland had been flooded with fake accounts. No directory operator ever risked working firms in his own country.

"Mine lived in Belgium. He had a cousin in the same business in

Spain, they had a working relationship with some friend in the United States."

"I want to know how it works," said Hannah.

Farise was the expert, but Gaunt could help with some of it, and wince in the process because he hadn't tumbled to it earlier.

Because it was simple. All a directory-fraud team needed was a small office, a good filing system, postage money—and names. That meant having a good, trusted field man who gathered technical journals, trade association lists, even genuine directories.

Then, as the harvest came in, the same field man travelled from his own safe base, moved the money fast from its bank account, shuffled it, lost it from sight.

They paused, and Hannah moistened her lips.

"Peter Fraser—"

"Was a damned good field man," said Gaunt gloomily.

Something else still troubled her. "Surely some firms complain, tell the police?"

"A few," said Farise and gestured his disgust. "Eventually—once they think about it. But by then the field man has his money and has moved on. Most companies who spot something wrong just tear up the evidence and throw it in a bucket. They've enough problems."

Gaunt sat silent for a moment. He was thinking of Peter Fraser, in Scotland, of the two hundred thousand pounds still in the Watermoor Milling bank account. The Watermoor account had to have been the end of the line, the last stage before the carefully laundered flow of money came home to Paul Weber.

But if Weber hadn't known exactly how Fraser operated, if Weber had been searching for that missing money for more than a year—yes, it could explain so much.

"Por favor," said Roberto Farise softly. "There is just one thing now. I can do nothing about this, our police can do nothing about this, not directly."

Hannah and Gaunt stared at him. Embarrassed, he prowled the hotel room for a moment then sighed.

"There is one very small line in these printed accounts, buried on the reverse side, under 'Business Conditions.' Can I tell you what it says? I don't even need to look. It reads 'This is an offer only, there is no obligation to pay.' It is enough—particularly when foreigners outside of Spain are the victims."

Gaunt swallowed. "That makes it legal?"

"Under Spanish law." Farise scowled. "No crime has been committed; the ruling comes from the highest authority."

"Then your 'highest authority' is an idiot," said Hannah.

"Sí." He went over, rested a hand on her shoulder, stroking gently and absently with his fingers. "I agree."

"Extradition?" Hannah frowned at his hand. "Bobi?"

"To Britain?" He shook his head. "You forget, Hannah. Your country and mine have no extradition agreement."

"So Weber has it made." Gaunt felt as if he'd been kicked in the stomach, hard. "Then why all the secrecy here?"

"That?" Farise seemed to have an unwilling answer ready for everything. "There could be different reasons. The obvious one is to avoid paying tax on it all. In his place, I would do the same—down to having a courier take those accounts by the suitcase-load to the mainland, and post them there."

"Couldn't you nail him on the tax angle?"

"On what evidence?" Farise's hand was still busy around Hannah's shoulder and straying from there. She seemed to have decided she liked it. "Jonny, I'm sorry. But the only person I could legally arrest is you. Trespass, breaking and entering, malicious damage, wounding—"

"How about grievous bodily harm to a Ministry of Justice official?" suggested Gaunt.

"No, that might get you a medal." Farise sighed, released his grip on Hannah, stood back, and stifled a yawn. "I need time to think, to work something out—and I may need help. All of us need some sleep. But the first problem is what Weber may do." He glanced at Hannah. "Can he sleep here?"

She nodded.

"Good." He grinned at Gaunt. "You're safe in this room—and fortunate. But don't step outside before you hear from me."

"How long will it take?" asked Gaunt.

"Perhaps a few hours." Farise headed for the door, reached it, then chuckled. "You know, I've never done this before, leaving a beautiful woman's bedroom in the middle of the night after asking her to let another man stay."

He opened the door and slipped out, and it closed gently. For a moment, Hannah sat where she was, a strange look in her eyes. Then she straightened, swallowed the last of the brandy in her paper cup, and set it down.

"Do you want to talk about it?" she asked.

Gaunt shook his head.

"Right." She became totally business-like. "The bed is big enough for two. You stay on your side, I'll stay on mine. One twitch in my direction and you'll wish you were dead."

"Hannah, I'm going to disappoint you," he said. "I'm damned tired. So climb back into your nightie: you're in no danger."

"I don't wear one," she said without thinking, then blushed. "Tell that when we get back to Edinburgh and—"

Gaunt grinned at her. She grinned back, flopped down as she was on the bed, and pointed at the other pillow.

"Go to hell, Jonny, but take your shoes off first."

She reached over and switched off the light.

They came at 4 A.M., so quietly that the first Gaunt knew was a hand over his mouth and the muzzle of a pistol against his ear. The bedside light clicked on and, hazily, he saw another figure leaning over Hannah, giving her the same treatment.

"*Lento* . . . slow and easy," murmured a voice he knew only too well.

The hand came away from his mouth, the muzzle of the pistol kept up its pressure. Gaunt sat upright, and Milo Bajadas gave him a mirthless grin.

"You and the woman." Bajadas didn't raise his voice. "You will get up, you will do exactly what you are told. You understand?"

Gaunt nodded. Reluctantly, Hannah did the same. The man holding the pistol to her head was a stranger. A third intruder was in the room, standing just inside the doorway, saying nothing, an hotel pass-key dangling in his left hand, the other deep in his pocket. The man took a step nearer the soft glow of the bedlight. It was John Cass, his long, thin face a stony mask, but a certain nervousness in the way he kept glancing around.

"What the hell is going on?" asked Hannah in a quiet, furious voice. "If this is some kind of a hold-up—" She stopped short as she received a back-handed cuff across the mouth from the man beside her.

"You and the woman will get up," repeated Bajadas patiently. "You will come with us. If either of you tries to escape then the other will be killed." The gun was removed from Gaunt's ear. "No more talking."

They were allowed to put on shoes. Then, dressed as they were, with pistols pressed against them, Gaunt and Hannah had to obey as they were led from the bedroom and along the dimly lit, deserted corridor to the elevators.

One elevator stood waiting, the door jammed open. Their three captors hustled them in, Cass unjammed the door, and Bajadas pressed the bottom button.

"We have a car in the garage," he said as the elevator door slid shut. "If you have any wild notions about the hotel staff, forget them. There is only the night porter at this hour, and he has—ah— decided to take a meal break."

"I like his timing," said Gaunt. He looked at Cass, who still seemed the most nervous of the three. "Getting in over your head, aren't you?"

"Shut up." Cass moistened his lips as the elevator rode down. "I wanted to finish you in Edinburgh—"

"You nearly did," said Gaunt unemotionally. "You may have crippled someone for life. Does that feel good?"

Cass stared at him. Then the elevator was sighing to a stop.

The door opened on the Agosto's basement garage. A grey Seat van was parked nearby, the rear door lying open.

"Wait," said Bajadas curtly. "Toni—"

They were pushed facing the side of the van and the man who had been Hannah's escort first tied her hands behind her back with some thin rope, then did the same with Gaunt. The rope was tight, and Bajadas grinned.

"Toni has a brother," he said curtly. "His brother was one of the plantation guards tonight. Remember that. Now get in."

They were shoved into the van, Cass and Bajadas following them.

The rear door closed, they heard the other man get behind the wheel, then the Seat's engine rumbled to life and they were moving.

"Where are you taking us?" asked Hannah wearily.

"Not far." Bajadas sat with his back against the metal panelling, the pistol in his hand held ready. "Then we can talk more comfortably, *sí?*"

The van only seemed to travel for a couple of minutes, then it came to a halt and the engine was switched off. A moment later, the rear door opened and they were pushed out.

It was still dark, and they were at the marina basin, on the concrete pier beside the *Black Bear*'s pontoon. There was no one else around, the only sounds were the creaking of mooring lines and the soft lapping of the water, but a chink of light showed in the sloop's cockpit.

"Go aboard," ordered Bajadas.

The pistol pressed against Gaunt's back jabbed him on. He reached the sloop's deck and stumbled awkwardly into the cockpit, and, as Hannah followed him, John Cass swung the cabin hatchway open. Down below, the cabin was brightly lit, the curtains were tightly closed—and Paul Weber stood waiting.

CHAPTER EIGHT

Unshaven, clad in a sweater and denim trousers, Paul Weber stood with his arms folded, his heavy face giving away little as Gaunt and Hannah were bundled down to join him. As John Cass and Bajadas followed, the man called Toni stayed in the cockpit and closed the hatch.

"Over there." Weber nodded towards the starboard couch, gave a slight, satisfied smile as his two prisoners were made to sit side by side, then glanced at Bajadas.

"Any trouble?"

Bajadas shook his head.

"Watch them."

Weber beckoned to Cass and led him over to the other end of the cabin; the two men talked briefly, their voices a murmur. Then Weber came back. His eyes were hard and angry, he held the crumpled account sheets from the plantation in one hand. He stuck them under Gaunt's nose.

"These were in her room." His voice was cold. "You took them of course?"

"Yes." There was no sense in denying it. He had left the sheets lying beside the bed. "But—"

"You're going to tell me she had nothing to do with it?" Weber sneered. "Don't. How do you think we found you so soon? She works with you, in the same office; Cass spotted her this morning, when she made that very convincing apartment inspection. He remembered seeing her when he came to visit you in Edinburgh." He turned to Hannah, eyeing her with reluctant admiration. "It was clever, sending a woman—but not clever enough. I can understand Cass remembering. Most men would."

"He doesn't look as though he'd be particularly interested," said Hannah sarcastically.

John Cass took an angry half-step towards her but Weber chuckled and waved him back, while Bajadas stifled a sly grin.

"Initial courtesies," said Weber, and switched his attention back to Gaunt. "I made some mistakes with your people. When you arrived in Tenerife, I still thought, hoped—" He shrugged. "I was wrong."

"It can happen." Gaunt chose his words carefully. Every instinct told him the only hope he and Hannah had left was to play for time, allow the Hispan boss to learn most of what he wanted, and cling to the thin chance that Captain Roberto Farise might still appear like some minor miracle. "It looks like we made our own mistakes."

"Sí." Weber sucked his lips. "I want to know why your department became suspicious, why you came here."

"First, your hired help were clumsy—too much muscle, too little brain." Gaunt gave a scathing glance at John Cass, who said nothing. "Then—well, we got lucky. We tripped over a bank account we hadn't known about, a bank account with a lot of money." He shrugged. "Find that much money, and something has to be wrong."

"I see." Weber made it a sigh. Then he suddenly, sharply, demanded, "What do you know about this boat?"

"Nothing." Gaunt shaped a puzzled look. "What about it?"

"Milo," said Weber softly.

Casually, Bajadas hit Gaunt across the side of the head with the barrel of his pistol. The blow sent Gaunt reeling and he collided into Hannah. Dazed, he forced himself upright again and saw Bajadas bring the weapon back for another blow.

"He's telling the truth," said Hannah desperately. "You wanted to buy the damned thing, it gave us a reason to be here."

Weber looked at her, then at Bajadas. He shook his head slightly and the pistol lowered.

"Thank you." The courtesy was sardonic. "So you came here, then tonight—how did you get out of that apartment, Gaunt?"

"The back way. There's a window."

Weber winced. "I should have thought. You had help, apart from this woman?"

Gaunt shrugged. "A squad or two of police, that's all."

"He's lying," snapped Cass.

"He has a sense of humour," corrected Weber. He leaned back against the cabin's central pillar of mast. "You see, Gaunt, money buys most things: if the Guardia Civil had been asked for help, I think I would have heard." His manner hardened. "Two men were seen at the plantation. You were one, who was the other?"

"Did it have to be another man?" asked Hannah.

Weber blinked, then recovered.

"Two people, then," he corrected himself and gave a slight, mock bow. "*Gracias.*"

"But plenty of people know we're in Puerto Tellas," reminded Gaunt. The rope biting into his wrists seemed to be getting tighter and he tried to ease it. "You can't ignore that."

"True," admitted Weber. "But I have to gamble that until tonight, until your performance at the plantation, you didn't know what was happening here."

"We do now," said Gaunt.

"*Sí*, which is the problem." Weber was in no hurry. Hands stuffed in his trouser pockets, he frowned at the deck. "When Peter Fraser died, this trouble began. He was almost my partner, he could be trusted"—his eyes flickered briefly to Cass—"despite what some others thought. He took an occasional extra percentage for himself, but that was incidental. One of his few faults was a lack of trust in others."

Hannah sniffed. "Even you?"

"Even me."

"So you didn't know how his money laundry worked?" she pressed determinedly.

"Just that we'd had a successful operation in southern England and Holland—and that he had collected before he died. We tried to trace it, tried hard." Weber shook his head. "Every way."

"I know," said Gaunt sarcastically. "Very hard."

The interruption was ignored by Weber. Bajadas seemed bored by it all, John Cass was fidgeting, as if anxious to move on.

"I sat with Fraser on this boat the last time he came to Tenerife." Weber watched Gaunt closely. "He was drunk, we quarrelled—and he threatened that if anything happened to him I'd regret it. He mumbled something about the boat being the key." He paused and pursed his lips. "Next day, everything was friendly again—but I didn't forget."

"I can't help. Maybe it was the brandy talking," said Gaunt wearily.

"I've searched, found nothing. Then I decided I had to get rid of the boat—but without fuss. Buying it was the easiest way." Weber looked around the cabin with distaste. "Now—I think I have a better idea."

"Fine, but leave us out of it," said Hannah aggressively. "British law can't touch you here; you know that. But what's the local law on kidnapping and assault?"

"Paul, I think she wants you to let them go," murmured Bajadas, and chuckled. "Señorita North, the problem is that you and your friend came at a bad time."

"Bad? It could get a lot worse." Hannah switched her glare to Cass, who was biting his lip. "You tell him. Or are you too scared?"

"Shut up." Cass took two nervous steps over, grabbed a handful of her hair, and twisted hard. "Just—shut up. Right?"

She kicked him, hard, in the stomach. Gasping, the man swung his fist and Gaunt jumped up, trying to get between them. He blocked the blow with his shoulder, then Hannah stared past him, eyes widening. Gaunt started to turn, then Bajadas's pistol barrel slammed against his head.

He felt an explosion of pain and heard Hannah cry out. Then the cabin blurred, whirled, and he plunged into a spinning darkness.

At first, it was as if he was still in a nightmare. He couldn't move, his head ached, he was only aware of a steady vibration going through his body and a low, background rumbling. He didn't know why, he wasn't sure that he cared.

But, gradually, his senses returned. He was in the cabin, he was alone, and he was lying on the cabin deck with his back propped against the mast pillar. His hands were still tied behind his back, but in addition several turns of rope round his chest now secured him to the mast.

The *Black Bear* was moving. The rumble and vibration came from her diesel, turning over at low revs. Powerless to do anything, he lay still and fought to clear his senses.

Where the hell was Hannah, what was happening to the sloop? As if in partial answer, the hull began a gentle, pitching roll which meant they were outside the marina breakwater and the engine note faded until it was barely ticking over.

Minutes later, the cockpit hatch grated open. He saw the grey light of early day, then Hannah was being pushed down to join him. Milo Bajadas was just behind her.

"Back with us?" Bajadas shoved Hannah aside, her hands still tied, then prodded Gaunt with his foot. "How's the head?"

Gaunt swore at him. Bajadas grinned, then turned his attention to Hannah. Handling her in a way which left her white-faced with anger, he forced her down on her knees, then shoved her over backwards. She landed heavily, stifled a gasp, and seemed beaten. She didn't struggle, didn't protest, as Bajadas, bending low, his long black hair brushing her legs, quickly tied her ankles together with a length of line, then tied a loose end round a metal stanchion.

"We do that with horses—anything that kicks," he said, rising again. "But I'll give you some light, make you more comfortable, eh?"

He went round the cabin, jerking the curtains open. More grey light flooded in, beginning to tinge with the first red glow of sunrise. Then, with a last glance around, he went back up the steps to the cockpit and the hatch slammed shut.

"Hannah," said Gaunt quietly.

She twisted round. Gaunt winced at the livid red mark which began just below her right eye and covered most of her cheek.

"Who did it?" he asked. "Cass?"

"No." She looked bitterly towards the cockpit. "That one. How about you?"

"I could use a new head." He waited, watching her squirm into a more comfortable position. The boat was still rolling gently and they were under way, but moving slowly. "What's happening? Where's Weber?"

"He left, with Cass." Hannah tried to inch nearer to him, but the line round her ankles brought her to a halt. "You were out for quite a while, Jonny. I thought you were dead—at first, anyway." She drew a deep breath and let it out as a sigh. "Right now we're sailing up and down off Puerto Tellas. They want an audience."

Puzzled, Gaunt stared at her.

"Why?"

"Because you and I have taken the *Black Bear* for a joy-ride." Hannah's voice was flat and tightly controlled. "That's after we spent a wild time in my room at the Agosto. You brought me down to the boat, we spent the rest of the night aboard it; why not? You represent the owners. Then we discover the engine works, and off we go." She saw Gaunt's incredulity. "It's going to look that way, Jonny. One or two people from the other boats saw us come out. There I was in the cockpit, with a smile on my face and a gun jammed in my navel."

Gaunt closed his eyes for a moment, his head thudding again.

"What's the rest of it?" he asked resignedly.

"The other one—the one they call Toni—can handle a boat. After a spell, we sail south down the coast. There's a cove, a bay of some kind, with deep water. Another boat will meet them there; the dinghy on this thing is in bad shape."

"Then they sink the *Black Bear*." Gaunt was surprised at how easy it was to be factual, unemotional. "What happens to us?"

"I wish I knew." Hannah said it softly. For a moment her eyes were on the view of the sunrise outside the spray-spattered glass. "I only heard some of it. But I do know about Weber—and Cass. We did hit them at a bad time. There's another directory mail-shot ready, a big one, and that's why Cass is here. He's shipping it out as personal luggage, scheduled service, on a midday flight to the mainland."

"And going with it?"

She nodded.

"Weber too?"

"At least to the airport." She grimaced and jerked her head towards the forepeak. "They heaved me in there. It wasn't too easy."

The cockpit hatch rasped open, Milo Bajadas stuck his head in and looked down at them. Satisfied, he vanished, the hatch slammed shut. The sloop made a slow, wallowing turn, then settled on a new course with the sunrise now to port instead of starboard.

"Grandstanding," said Hannah unemotionally.

Gaunt nodded.

He felt miserably helpless in a way that had nothing to do with the way his head ached. There had to be something he could do, now or later, whenever the chance came.

If it came, he told himself grimly. When he moved, the rope round his chest scraped his damaged ribs. The way his wrists were tied, any attempt to free them was futile.

Hannah had begun a laborious attempt to sit upright. He watched her struggle, finally succeed, then lie back, exhausted, dishevelled, her clothing torn and in disorder, her head resting against the couch. Henry Falconer would have been proud of her.

He almost said it aloud, then changed his mind.

The rest came down to what Paul Weber intended to do with them. In the short term—yes, he and Hannah might be useful alive, a bargaining counter if anything went unexpectedly wrong. But after that—Gaunt pursed his lips at the thought. After that they would be a liability, nothing more. A liability to be eliminated.

Even that was looking on the bright side. He and Hannah had only one card left to play, and that was Captain Roberto Farise. Maybe they should have played Farise's existence earlier, maybe it was already too late.

"Hannah." He said her name softly and waited until she looked up. "We've still got Bobi, haven't we?"

"Yes." A faint hope flared in her eyes. "I nearly told them. I wanted to, but—"

She stopped. The *Black Bear*'s diesel had begun to quicken, not in a rush but gradually, purposefully. Then she began to alter course again. Craning his neck, forcing himself as far upright as he could, Gaunt tried to keep the sun in sight. They were heading out of the bay, sailing almost due west.

For spectators ashore, the picture would be complete. The sloop, taken out on a stupid adventure by two foreigners, had last been seen heading out from land.

To disappear, as far as Puerto Tellas was concerned. Leaving the way clear to sneak back farther down the coast and rendezvous as Paul Weber had arranged.

The pitching motion grew worse, spray regularly drenching the cabin roof as the thirty-horsepower diesel plugged on at cruising speed. The next time Bajadas opened the hatch to check on his prisoners he looked grey and unhappy while, behind him, Gaunt had a glimpse of white-topped waves and the other man lounging unperturbed at the wheel.

About an hour passed. Then the *Black Bear* changed course again and began a south-east heading, one that would take her back in towards the island.

Hannah had been sitting head bowed, legs doubled under her, jammed against the couch. For a while, Gaunt left her alone and heard her give an occasional mutter or a soft curse. But, at last, he felt it had gone on too long.

"Can anyone join in?" he asked.

She sighed, squirmed round, and showed him what she'd been doing. The small dress ring on the index finger of her right hand had a blue stone in a claw setting and she was using it like a blunt knife, fraying away at the ropes around her feet.

"It's better than doing nothing," she said and tried to smile. "I should have worn my diamonds."

"Next time," said Gaunt wryly.

She grimaced and looked around the cabin.

"Any other time, I'd have said this was a really nice boat," she said almost absently. "Her last trip anywhere; it's a waste."

"I suppose so." It was a thought Gaunt would have placed very low in his own priorities, but he sensed she meant it. "You know about boats?"

"A little. There was someone I knew, years ago." Whatever the memory, she banished it. "Back to work."

Wriggling round, she resumed her stubborn task.

Bajadas didn't look in on them again for some time. When he did, the sloop had already made another change of course and the sea seemed to have moderated. He came down, glanced at them, grunted, then returned to the cockpit. Soon after the hatch had closed, Gaunt had a glimpse of land as the sloop rolled. They were in the shelter of a long, rocky headland, apparently sailing parallel with it.

Suddenly, Hannah gave a soft gasp of triumph. He looked over, in time to see her elbow her way up from the deck, stand for a moment with the parted rope lying at her feet, then sit on the couch. He gave her a quick, warning frown.

"Careful."

She nodded, moving her feet with relief, getting the circulation back into them, wincing at what that did. After a couple of minutes she rose, balancing awkwardly with her wrists still tied behind her, and came over.

"Try," she invited, kneeling beside him.

Gaunt's fingers managed to touch the knotted rope around her wrists. But he had no real feeling in them, no strength he could use. He gave up, and Hannah tried in turn, working blindly at his knots, swearing under her breath with equal frustration.

"I can't." She shook her head, stopped to draw breath, then stiffened as the steady note of the diesel took a sudden change, slowing.

"Take a look," Gaunt told her.

Nodding, Hannah got up, peered out of the nearest cabin window, then dropped down beside him again.

"We're turning, going into some kind of bay." She grimaced. "There's damn all to see but cliffs and rock."

So they had arrived. Gaunt listened to the diesel as it continued to slow until it was doing little more than murmur. He could see the tops of cliffs on both sides of the boat, which was still creeping in.

"Try again," he suggested.

She did, stayed for a long moment just staring, then returned and crouched down, her voice low.

"It's the way they said. There's a small boat coming from the shore." Her eyes met his own and Gaunt knew the effort she was making to keep control. "Jonny, suppose I said I was scared?"

"I'd be glad of the company."

The diesel stopped, the sloop began drifting, and they could hear the faint putter of the other boat's engine as it came near. Bajadas shouted from the cockpit, a voice answered his hail, and Hannah was back on the deck, beside the couch again, as the hatchway opened.

Toni, not Bajadas, came down and paused for a moment. He was a small man, lightly built, swarthy, shabby, the kind of man who had hard eyes and showed no particular intelligence. He had a pistol stuck in his belt and hardly glanced at them as he headed aft, along the narrow companionway that led to the diesel compartment. Almost immediately there was the sound of hammering, metal against metal. When it stopped, he returned, grinned deliberately in Hannah's direction, and went back up to the cockpit.

Another sound joined the mutter of the approaching boat engine and the soft slap of the sea against the sloop's hull, a gurgling, bubbling sound which made Gaunt's blood run cold. He glanced at Hannah and, from her face, she also understood. The sea water intake for the diesel's cooling jacket had been smashed, the sea was beginning to gush in.

It would take a few minutes for the *Black Bear* to sink, but nothing would stop that now.

The hatch had been left open, he could see empty blue sky as he strained again at the ropes which tied him. Then, unexpectedly, Milo Bajadas came clattering down into the cabin. He stopped, put his hands on his hips, and gave a chuckle.

"*Qué pasa?* Don't you want to come with us?" Still amused, he pulled a knife from his pocket, clicked open the spring blade, then cut the rope which secured Gaunt to the mast pillar. He approached Hannah with more caution, shaped a silent whistle of surprise as he saw her feet were free, and drew his gun. "Okay, out—both of you. The woman first."

Hannah went up, reached the cockpit, and was shoved out from there by Toni, pushed along the deck.

"Now you." Bajadas gave a nervous glance at a thin pool of water beginning to spread into the cabin from aft, kicked Gaunt to his feet, and pushed him towards the steps. "Move."

Gaunt obeyed, stumbled into the cockpit. The high, barren cliffs had the sea lapping at their base, the boat almost alongside was a small, battered fishing dinghy with an outboard engine.

He took another step clear of the hatchway, then realised Bajadas's swarthy companion was still out on the deck, frowning at the dinghy in a puzzled uncertain way. There were two aboard it, a man sitting near the bow with his back towards them, the other, handling the tiller, a small figure in baggy overalls and a floppy hat. An untidy hummock of old canvas lay between them in the centre thwarts.

"*Hola.*" Toni stiffened and shouted in alarm. "Wait—"

He started to fumble for his pistol.

Jammed open to full throttle, the outboard engine poured a burst of blue exhaust and the dinghy crashed against the sloop's hull. As it happened, the man at the bow swung round and leapt across. It was Miguel Reales, and the shotgun he was gripping by the barrels swung in a short, vicious arc which smashed the butt down on his swarthy opponent's gun-arm. There was a snap of bone. Toni screamed.

The small figure at the dinghy's stern gave a short chirping whistle. The canvas hummock exploded to life and a lean, brown, four-legged shape took a single, standing jump to land snarling in the cockpit exactly as Bajadas came scrambling through the hatch.

Eyes wide with fear, Bajadas triggered the pistol in his hand. The shot clipped the big German shepherd dog's left ear, then the animal sprang, knocking him over, those great white-toothed jaws closing like a trap on the man's shoulder, shaking and worrying him like a rag doll.

A second chirping whistle came from the dinghy. Growling, Oro let go but stayed where he was, teeth bared and menacing only inches away from Bajadas's terrified face. His gun had fallen. Gaunt kicked it aside, then stared as the small figure in the dinghy tossed aside her hat and grinned up at him.

"Marta—" He swallowed hard, then glanced along the deck. The other man was cowering, his one good arm trembling in surrender above his head, and Miguel was using a knife to cut Hannah free.

Seconds later, it was his turn. As the ropes fell away, Miguel slapped him on the back and turned to the dinghy.

"Okay, little one?" he asked.

"*Sí.*" She was using the engine to keep the dinghy against the sloop's hull. "*Hola,* Jonny; are you all right?"

"Fine—now." He found it hard to even think for a moment, then Hannah was beside him, looking equally dazed. He put an arm round her shoulders, hugged her, and felt her shudder with relief.

"Jonny." Marta called to him again from the dinghy. "You look like you're sinking. Better not waste time."

She was right. The *Black Bear* was already lower in the water and beginning to show a list to starboard.

Miguel had collected Bajadas's pistol. First they helped Hannah down into the dinghy, then made Toni follow and sit near the bow. Gaunt went next, then, moaning, crawling on hands and knees, his mauled, torn shoulder oozing blood, Bajadas somehow followed with Miguel close behind.

Marta gave another of those shrill, chirping whistles and Oro barked once, then sprang down to join them. The girl moved the tiller and opened the outboard's throttle and they swung clear.

The *Black Bear* died slowly, reluctantly, settling gradually until her deck was awash. But the end was a bubbling gout of air and she slid under the surface, leaving a brief white disturbance which vanished within seconds in the light swell.

Gaunt saw something very close to tears in Marta's eyes. He reached over, squeezed her hand, then glanced at Miguel.

"Deep water?"

"Very deep." Miguel pantomimed a chasm with one hand. "We call this bay El Diablo Gris—the Grey Devil." He scowled at their two prisoners. Their only interest now seemed to be the big, dark brown dog watching them closely, growling deep in its throat. "They chose well: even fishermen avoid coming near." He saw the question shaping on Gaunt's lips. "*Sí.* We did. But suppose we get ashore first. Okay, little one?"

Marta opened the outboard's throttle again, and the dinghy's bow came round towards the shore.

There was a hidden gap in the cliffs farther up the narrow bay, and a small shingle beach. The dinghy grounded there, they splashed ashore, and Oro was more than enough of a guard for their two injured, openly terrified prisoners. A rough track began just above the shingle and a glinting Ford truck was parked among the rocks.

"Two more for the collection, Señor Gaunt." Miguel Reales thumbed casually at the underside of the truck. Trussed hand and foot, two men in fishing overalls lay there in the shade, on their backs, their faces resigned and gloomy. "First, of course, we let them unload the dinghy, get it down to the water. Then, the dog and I came along, said a simple *por favor*—and they obliged."

"That part I'll believe." Rubbing his wrists, getting the last of the circulation flowing again, Gaunt was just beginning to accept the reality of what had happened. "Where's your father? How is he now?"

"Our *médico* friend removed a bullet from his arm." Miguel smiled at the memory. "He roared like a bull, but it was only a flesh wound. I had to force him not to come with us; he needs rest."

"Make sure he gets it." Gaunt drew a deep breath. "Now, how did you know to be here?"

"Ask the little one." Miguel nodded in Marta's direction. "I just did what she asked."

Marta was perched on a long, flat rock and Hannah sat beside her. The bruise on Hannah's face was beginning to blacken, she looked tired and drained, but she smiled as they came over.

"Tell them about it, little one," invited Miguel. He took a casual glance towards the beach, where Oro had now hunkered down and was eyeing the former crew of the *Black Bear* balefully. "It's your story."

Marta frowned and looked troubled. She had got rid of the old overalls she'd worn over her shorts and shirt, and Gaunt saw she was still wearing the gold pendant and chain which had been Peter Fraser's gift.

"Tell me what will happen to Paul first." Her young face was earnest. "Jonny, I know what he might have done to you—and your friend. But—"

"He's family, your stepbrother," said Hannah softly. "But sometimes people have to choose, Marta. Life's like that."

Marta looked at Hannah gratefully and gave a slow nod.

"It was early this morning—very early, at sunrise. Oro wakened me; he sleeps in my room. He was growling, I heard voices, so I got up and dressed." She moistened her lips. "It was Paul and that man, Cass. They were talking, and Paul sounded angry."

"So you listened?" encouraged Gaunt.

"*Sí.*" She gave a slightly shamefaced nod. "They were talking about you, about sinking the *Black Bear*, and the story they would tell afterwards. Paul said two of his men could take a dinghy by road to El Diablo Gris, and that there was a lot he and Cass had to do before they went to the airport."

"Did he say what would happen to us?"

"I didn't hear." She avoided his eyes for a moment.

"It doesn't matter." Gaunt sensed she was lying, but it didn't matter. Gently, he prodded her on. "What did you do then?"

"I—I couldn't have gone to the Guardia Civil. But you'd said you knew Miguel and Tomás. So I went to the Bar Tomás and told them." Marta combed a hand through her long, dark hair, bit her lip, and for a moment looked very vulnerable. "I knew Paul wouldn't notice whether I'd gone or not."

Part in sympathy, part agreeing, Miguel made an awkward business of clearing his throat.

"Because it was Marta, we believed her," he said gruffly. "There was not time to be clever about anything, Señor Gaunt. My father told me to take his car, and we got out here. We"—he grinned—"she said she was coming, and with that monster she calls a dog beside her, who argues?"

"Nobody." Hannah impulsively hugged the small figure beside her. Then she glanced at Gaunt. "If they're still heading for the airport—"

He nodded. "Miguel, I want to borrow your car. Can you stay and look after things here?"

"*Sí.*" Miguel brought a car key from his pocket and tossed it over. "We left it farther up the track. Just remember it belongs to my father."

"I will." Gaunt glanced at Hannah. "What about you?"

She shook her head. "I'll be more useful here. And I don't feel fit to be seen anywhere."

He grinned, winked at Marta, and set off up the track.

The car, an old, well-polished Ford, was parked in the shade of some stunted trees about a quarter of a mile up the track. The interior was spotless, a small vase filled with flowers was attached to the fascia, and the engine started at the first turn of the key.

Gaunt set it moving, the sheer, ordinary comfort of the driving seat feeling like luxury as the Ford jolted its way over the rough surface, leaving the cliffs of the Grey Devil behind.

He had to drive for a mile before the track joined a road, where he made a left turn towards Puerto Tellas.

The track had been bad, the road wasn't much better. It wound through a dark lava rock landscape where the only sign of life was the squashed body of a large grey lizard, killed on the road by some previous vehicle. Holding tight to the steering-wheel, keeping the old Ford bouncing and rattling along, he thought grimly of the surprise in store for Paul Weber.

With a new blizzard of directory fraud mail-shot accounts ready to go, the Hispan boss had to feel he'd escaped. He was operating in an area where the returns came high, where crooked fortunes could be made overnight with unbelievable ease. It was the kind of crime which played the percentage game—the high percentage of business where routine was all that mattered.

The car bucked over a pot-hole. He swore to himself, still thinking about the directory operators, the stories he had heard.

One worked a variation, sending out a dummy cover with his fraudulent account. The cover showed an advertisement for one of the world's largest oil companies, one the oil company knew nothing about. Another, working out of South Africa, had expanded his net to include a police forces section and had driven one English police financial controller to the brink of a raging fury. It was a world where trickery reigned, the legal loopholes between countries were highways to riches, and the international postal and banking systems were unwitting allies.

Even just a few years history of directory mail-shots behind him would mean that Paul Weber was already a very rich man. One about to become richer.

The road ribboned on. Then, without warning, a small one-pump filling station, little more than a roadside shack, appeared ahead. Why it was there and whom it served didn't matter. It had a telephone pole and wires. Gaunt pulled in, and the old woman in charge put down her knitting, let him into a fly-infested back room, and allowed him to use her precious *teléfono*.

He dialled the Hotel Agosto's number, got through, and asked the switchboard for Roberto Farise's room, and a moment later the Ministry of Justice captain was on the line.

"You!" Farise sounded startled when he heard Gaunt's voice. "Where the hell are you, and where's Hannah? Both of you disappear, the sloop has gone—"

"Keep it till I get to you," Gaunt stopped him. "Hannah is on the beach at El Diablo Gris, south along the coast. She's sitting on four of Weber's people. Can you get help to her?"

"She's all right?"

"Yes."

"Wait," Farise spoke sharply to someone else in his room, then came back on the line. "And the boat?"

"Sank by arrangement."

"I understand." Farise said it bleakly. "I also understand a few other things now. Anything else?"

"Weber."

"*Sí.* We know where he is, and Tenerife is still an island."

"We?" asked Gaunt, brushing away some of the nearest flies.

"I brought in some of my own men." Farise broke off again to have another brief discussion with whoever was with him. "Two are leaving now for El Diablo Gris. If we have real charges against Weber—"

"They're real," said Gaunt sarcastically. "But I'd like to be there. Where will you be?"

"Not at the Agosto. Too many people would think you were a ghost." Farise chuckled. "The marina; make it there. You know my car."

Gaunt hung up, escaped from the flies, and thanked the old woman on the way out. She didn't look up from her knitting.

It was twenty minutes later when he reached Puerto Tellas and turned in at the marina. Roberto Farise's sleek Lancia was parked on its own in the sunlight and Gaunt stopped the Ford beside it, crossed over, and slid into the passenger seat beside Farise.

"This is Sergeant Pinar." Farise gestured towards the large wooden-faced man in civilian clothes who sat behind them, his head touching the roof. Then he looked Gaunt over. "A bad time?"

"It had its moments." Gaunt watched him start the car. "Where are we going?"

"The airport, I think." Farise set the Lancia moving as he spoke. "Weber and his friend Cass left the Villa Hispan about five minutes ago, by car. They had three large suitcases aboard. Before that, they were at the plantation and at the Hispan office in the Agosto." Driving unhurriedly, he gave Gaunt a sideways glance. "Don't worry. I have a car tailing them, and the airport has been warned."

"Then you were going to pull them in?"

"Maybe, for questioning." Farise shrugged. "But when you and Hannah disappeared—that made the difference."

"I'm glad," said Gaunt. "Hannah will feel that way too."

"You think so?" Farise gave him an anxious frown. "I'd like that. She is a splendid woman."

They left Puerto Tellas behind and gathered speed on the main road for the airport, Farise asking questions while he drove.

"I didn't think," he exploded at last, thumping a fist against the steering wheel. "I shouldn't have left you in that hotel room—"

"I'd have done it that way," Gaunt soothed, then realised Farise had stopped his outburst and was frowning ahead.

They were coming up to a road junction. The Aeropuerto sign pointed left, but the junction was a jam of halted traffic and a thin pillar of smoke climbed skywards just beyond the turn. People were out of the other vehicles, standing and staring, but doing nothing.

Tight-lipped, silent, Farise coasted the Lancia as near as he could and stopped, and they got out. A man in a grey suit hurried over to them, spoke quickly and quietly to Farise, then shrugged at Sergeant Pinar.

"Jonny." Farise swallowed hard and beckoned.

They walked to the junction. The edge of the road fell away to one side, a gentle slope ending in a patch of scrub.

Paul Weber's white Mercedes, or what was left of it, lay upside-down and smouldering at the bottom. Pieces of bodywork were strewn on the road and the slope, the car looked as though it had been torn apart, and everywhere the ground was littered with fragments of paper.

"They're still in it," said Farise dully. "It was a bomb of some kind, as they turned. At least we know who they were; it isn't easy now."

One of the fragments of papers fluttered against his feet. He stooped, glanced at it, then handed it to Gaunt. It was the singed remains of a telex directory account.

"Yours," said Farise. "And the rest is mine."

He turned and shouted for his men.

It was early evening before Gaunt got to Hannah in her hotel room. Part of the time he'd been with Farise, while the two shattered bodies were recovered from the wrecked Mercedes and police experts moved in. A Guardia Civil officer in uniform, a stranger, had

wanted statements but Farise had waved that aside. They had gone
to the plantation, then the Villa Hispan. Between them, they'd
uncovered enough evidence to show just how big Paul Weber's operation had been.

Though it was finished now . . . he thought.

A few more of Weber's team had been arrested and Milo Bajadas,
his mauled shoulder swathed in bandages, was alternating between
weeping and shouting for a lawyer.

At last, Farise had work of his own to do, police and other agitated officials to meet. Gaunt got a lift in a police car back to his
apartment and, as he went in, noticed that the old Ford had gone
from the marina parking-lot. He showered, freshened up, helped
himself to a stiff brandy from the refrigerator's stock, then walked
across to the Agosto and took the elevator up to Hannah's room.

She opened the door, looked at him silently for a moment, then
nodded and beckoned him in.

"Marta's here," she said quietly. "She knows, and we've talked a
lot."

He saw Hannah had almost totally hidden the bruise on her face
with make-up. She had changed her clothes, her hair was brushed
back; if he hadn't known, hadn't seen, it would have been hard to
relate her to the woman who'd come ashore with him.

"You look good," he said, meaning it.

She smiled and led him through. Marta was out on the balcony,
Oro dozing at her feet. She had been crying, her eyes were still red,
but she was composed.

"I'm sorry, Marta," said Gaunt, bending over her.

"*Gracias*, Jonny." She looked up, took his face in her two small
hands, and kissed him on the cheek. "Hannah explained. It wasn't
your fault."

Oro gave a questioning growl. As Gaunt stood back, the dog rose
and laid its large head on the child's lap.

"Jonny." Hannah beckoned him back into the room, away from
the balcony. "You've seen this?"

She was holding Marta's gold pendant in her hand. He nodded.

"Fraser gave her it."

"You told me." She spoke quietly, but with a strange excitement.

"He got it in New York, at Tiffany's. That didn't mean anything to you?"

He shook his head.

"It wouldn't, I suppose—not to you." She almost laughed. "Remember what Weber told us, that Fraser made a threat?"

"About the boat—"

"He was wrong. Or at least, he had the wrong boat." Hannah shoved the pendant nearer. "This shows a boat, doesn't it? And you know what's on the back?"

"The Tiffany name, and a hallmark." He tried to understand her but was lost.

"This is a custom-made piece of jewellery," she said patiently. "And that's not just a hallmark; it's a design number."

"So?" Gaunt stared at her, with the faint beginnings of an idea.

"So one thing you should know about Tiffany's is that they keep a register. You can even get a gold tag from them, for a few dollars, and you're on that register—your name, any address you want to give, and wherever that piece of jewellery or even that tag comes up, they'll contact you."

Gaunt swallowed. "What kind of an address?"

"That's what I've spent half the afternoon trying to find out—through Edinburgh, because Henry has the contacts." She paused, swinging the pendant by its chain, looking out towards the balcony. "It's a Swiss bank account, numbered. Give them the pendant design number, and that's enough—and it's in the name of Peter Fraser or, failing, Marta Maria Weber."

"Legal?"

"Legal. They say there's about half a million Swiss francs and a safe deposit box." Hannah shook her head in near-disbelief. "And you know the Swiss: nobody will ever be able to prove where it came from."

"Who's going to try?" Gaunt drew a deep breath. "Will you?"

"Me?" She shook her head. "I'm just someone's private secretary. Will I tell Marta?"

"Later." Gaunt was thinking of Edinburgh, of someone else who mattered. "Hannah, when you talked to Henry—"

"The Canadian girl?" Hannah's smile faded a little and she hesitated. "Jonny, I asked. She's all right, she'll walk. But—"

"Well?"

Hannah shrugged. "I don't think she quite told you everything. There's—well, another friend. He flew in from Canada yesterday, he's talking about marrying her as soon as she's able to leave. You— Well, that's how it happens."

"That's how it happens," agreed Gaunt.

Then he found he was grinning. Hannah looked alarmed.

"I just thought of something," he said wryly. "You know what it means? I've just escaped the Fraser family tree."

He had a more difficult time later that evening at the local Guardia Civil post, across a wooden table from Roberto Farise.

"I have a story that is half a story," said Farise. "There are blanks even Hannah says she cannot fill—and I have to believe her."

"Blanks?" asked Gaunt.

"Blanks," repeated Farise. "First, there was what happened at Weber's plantation. An explosion—and his men swear two men were involved. But your story is you went alone, and there may have been some kind of fire. Correct?"

"That's the way I remember it," said Gaunt.

"And this man Miguel Reales, who rescued you both; you say you met him by chance?"

Gaunt nodded. "His father runs a bar."

"I know that!" Farise slapped the table hard, indignantly. "The same way I know a few other things—and guess more."

"Like what?"

"I'll stay with fact. The bomb aboard Weber's car was small, powerful, probably a military grenade of some kind. It was activated by a simple radio remote-control device, short-range, but effective.

"So someone could pick and choose his spot," murmured Gaunt. "Make sure no one else was hurt?"

"Nice and civilised," agreed Farise sarcastically. "And perhaps this same someone also knew Weber was going to the airport, would have to pass that way. Fortunately, I know exactly what you were doing—I think." He rested his head in his hands for a moment, then looked up. "Jonny, I intend to report that a man like Paul Weber had many enemies, many criminal rivals. That I believe one of these rivals was responsible, but there is no chance of tracing him. You understand?"

"I think so," said Gaunt cautiously.

"You damn well do." Farise sat back, folded his arms, and scowled. But there was a faint twinkle in his eyes. "In return, you do something for me—for both of us. You were due to fly back tomorrow?"

Gaunt nodded.

"Then damned well be on that plane, before someone with slightly greater intelligence decides to ask you more questions."

"I think you can count on it, Bobi," said Gaunt.

He held out his hand. Farise grinned and gripped it.

The Guardia Civil post was in the old village. Although it was close to midnight when he left, the Bar Tomás was still open. There were only a few customers, and Miguel was behind the bar.

Gaunt sat at a table. After a couple of minutes Miguel came over with a bottle of brandy and a glass.

"A drink, señor?" Gravely, he filled the glass to the brim.

"Have one yourself," invited Gaunt.

"*Gracias,* maybe later." The young islander spoke loudly. "You see, my father had this accident to his arm—unimportant, but painful. So he stayed at home and I am on my own tonight."

"I'm leaving tomorrow," said Gaunt quietly. "I came to thank you—both of you."

"No need."

"And to ask a question." Gaunt sipped the brandy and watched Miguel over the rim. "How did he do it?"

"Do what, señor?" Miguel frowned at the table, produced a cloth, and rubbed at an imaginary spot. "My father will be off work for a few days, but he won't mind. It will give him some extra time for his hobby."

"His hobby?" Gaunt raised an eyebrow.

"*Sí.*" Miguel tucked the cloth away. "He repairs old toys, then gives them to the Church for the poor—clockwork toys, mechanical toys, even sometimes the clever ones that work with batteries and little radios. He enjoys his hobby, Señor Gaunt."

"A man needs an interest." Gaunt finished his drink at a long, single gulp and rose. "Give your father my regards."

Hannah saw him off at Reina Sofia airport the next morning. So did Farise, who made a fierce mumble about coming along to make sure, then stayed in the background.

Hannah was staying on. Only for a few days, she'd told Falconer by phone. She needed time to recover, there were some small details she could tidy.

Or that was her story. She waved goodbye from the terminal building as Gaunt boarded the Iberia jet for the flight to London. Roberto Farise was at her elbow.

Gaunt settled back as the plane took off and climbed.

There was no need to tell Falconer too much about Farise. He had worries enough.

A stewardess came along with the previous day's British newspapers. Gaunt took one, ordered a whisky from the bar, and started to turn to the financial pages.

He needed a new car, it was going to cost money. Something was niggling at the back of his mind about tin shares.

And he couldn't afford gold.

ABOUT THE AUTHOR

Noah Webster is the pseudonym of a popular and prolific mystery writer who is known for the unusual locales of his novels. This is the eighth novel to feature Jonathan Gaunt, who was introduced to Crime Club readers in *Flickering Death*. Recent Jonathan Gaunt adventures include *A Problem in Prague*, *An Incident in Iceland*, and *A Pay-off in Switzerland*. The author lives in Scotland with his wife. They have three children.

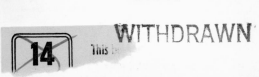